# L'Archevêque

*Based on a true story*

## Written by

## William Alan Larsh

Copyright © 2016 by William Alan Larsh

*L'Archevêque*

by William Alan Larsh

Library of Congress Control Number: 2016918281

CreateSpace Independent Publishing Platform, North Charleston, North Carolina

Printed by CreateSpace, an Amazon.com Company.

Available from Amazon.com and other retail outlets.

ISBN-13: 978-1537598963

www.createspace.com

Cover art from an original oil painting by Cynthia Lynn Larsh; illustrated map and Larsh Family Tree by Cynthia Lynn Larsh.

Bible quotations are taken from the King James Holy Bible, printed by G.E. Eyre and W. Spottiswoode, London, England, 1851.

*To my wife, Cindy, for her creative input.*

*To my daughter, Mary, for her expert editing.*

*To my son, Ethan, for his encouragement.*

*To my sister, Donna, a true L'Archevêque, for her help with my French and English.*

*And to my Mom and Dad in heaven, forever with me.*

# Preface

This novel is based on the true story of the life of a French fur trader in the Ohio Valley during the mid-1700s. His name was Paul L'Archevêque. Not much was known about him in his early life other than he was from Canada and his ancestors migrated to Canada from France. He led a brave and courageous life in the wilderness of the New World. He left Canada as a young man, leaving the safety of his family and home in Montreal to become a fur trader with the Shawnee Indians in the Ohio Valley. His interaction with the Shawnee Indians would forever have a profound effect on his life.

Paul L'Archevêque was fearless, independent, and he was, in the truest sense of the word, a frontiersman. He was not a famous frontiersman, such as Daniel Boone, nor did his life have any real historical significance. Nonetheless, he was in every respect the same kind of hero as Daniel Boone.

His life story was that of a seemingly average man who one might consider to be the archetypical pioneer in early America. He led his life through his own daring, rugged individualism, and a continuous struggle for survival. Paul L'Archevêque was indeed an ordinary man who led an extraordinary life,

contributing in his own small way to the making
of America.

**EUROPEAN SETTLEMENTS AND INDIAN TRIBES - 1750**

# Chapter 1

Paul L'Archevêque was born in Montreal, Canada, in 1734. The L'Archevêque family had lived in the Montreal area for generations. Paul was the son of a cobbler, Paul Phillipe L'Archevêque, who was born in Montreal in 1711. His mother, Angelique LeBoeuf, was also from Montreal. His grandparents and great-grandparents were all born in Montreal. Claude L'Archevêque, his great-great-grandfather, had been the first L'Archevêque to leave France and settle in the New World.

Although little was known about Paul L'Archevêque's early life, he apparently led an uneventful and perfectly normal childhood. His parents were hardworking people and provided for Paul and his younger sister and brother. Paul worked throughout his early life with his father, making and repairing shoes. It was expected of him to continue in the family business, not because it was all that successful, but because it was what Paul and his father knew how to do.

The L'Archevêques were a cog in the wheel of the Montreal community. They were devout, church-going people, trudging to Mass on Sunday with the rest of the largely Catholic population. The father provided a beneficial service to the town, opening shop early every

4

morning, Monday through Saturday, and closing at seven every night. Paul, however, had other ideas regarding his future. He was a restless youth who longed for something more exciting out of life. By his late teens, Paul had grown into a tall, blue-eyed, handsome, muscular young man with rugged features and wavy brown hair.

Many young girls in Montreal were attracted to him. A few of the girls from the church parish had come around with cakes and pastries in an attempt to win his heart. The girls were cute and sweet. He knew that if he gave in to their charms, he would be stuck in Montreal forever. His dreams of adventure and any hope of escape from the endless monotony of his present life would be dashed. He needed to leave soon before he gave in to the temptations the girls offered.

Paul's first cousin, Antoine LeBoeuf, his mother's brother's son, had departed Montreal three years before to travel west to the French settlement of Kaskaskia in the Illinois Territory on the Mississippi River. Paul had been very close to Antoine throughout their childhood, even though Antoine was three years older than Paul. Paul was deeply disappointed that he had been unable to leave with Antoine. Paul was only sixteen years old at the time and his parents had forbidden it. Out of respect for his aunt and uncle, Antoine convinced Paul to wait until he got older. After having been gone a year, Antoine had finally written to Paul describing his new life and newfound fortune as a fur trader in Kaskaskia. Antoine enclosed a map so that if Paul was eventually able to join him, he would find his way more easily.

The fur trade was thriving in Canada and America in the 1700s. In Kaskaskia, it was a booming commercial venture, profiting many. The French were competing with the British for trade in the New World, especially the fur trade. Felt hats made from beaver pelts were the rage among European men. Mink, fox, and otter pelts had also become valuable commodities. The opportunity for enterprising, brave young men, such as Antoine and Paul, had arrived. The idea of becoming a fur trader was adventurous to Paul as well. He had done nothing but dream about leaving home for three years since his cousin left.

Now that Paul was a fully-grown man, he finally worked up the nerve again to tell his father he wanted to leave Montreal. His father understood Paul wanting to venture out on his own. He had seen Paul's restlessness and his lack of enthusiasm working in the shoe shop over the last few years. His father was of course disappointed, but nevertheless gave his son his blessing. His mother was devastated at the news of his leaving, but her emotions soon subsided, and she too wished him well. Both parents knew of Paul's adventurous and independent spirit and could do nothing to deter him from leaving, especially now that he was of age.

The journey from Montreal to Kaskaskia would be a long, arduous trip for Paul, more than thirteen hundred miles over land and water. Although most of it would be traveled by canoe, some of the trip would be hiked on foot heading south from Lake Ontario through the Allegheny Mountains. The trip began from Montreal down the St. Lawrence River to Lake Ontario in a canoe he had already dug out from a birch tree years before. After many days making his way down the river and across Lake Ontario, he reached upstate New York. He abandoned his canoe, removing all the necessary supplies, including his musket, gunpowder, several rounds of ammunition, a knife, an axe, two pieces of flint, beef jerky, and his bedroll.

He hated discarding the canoe. Paul built it with his own two hands when he was only fifteen years old. It had taken him months to carve it out and sand it down to smooth perfection. It pained him to leave it behind. The canoe had represented his long-awaited goal to leave Montreal over the last several years.

As much as he wanted to take it with him on his journey, he knew he could not conceivably carry it with him over the mountains.  He took a moment of deep reflection as he pushed the canoe back into Lake Ontario.  Paul hoped that maybe some young adventurous boy, like he himself had been, might eventually find it.

After days of hiking over the Allegheny Mountain Range, he located the Allegheny River from the map that his cousin sent him.  He was lucky not to have come across any hostile Iroquois Indians, as they were prevalent in that area of the country.  He was exhausted, but he worked up the strength to cut down a birch tree and dig out another canoe.  It had been years since he built his last one, but he had neither the time nor the inclination to carve out one matching the quality of his prized canoe.  He could not take months to work on it.  He tried his best to find the right rocks to sand down the rough spots in the wood, but it would never be as smooth or as comfortable as the one he abandoned.

Paul spent two and a half days working on it.  Although lacking the proper tools, the canoe proved satisfactory to Paul upon its completion.  He carved out an oar from a large branch to help him navigate.  Paul believed that his new canoe, although rudimentary in its craftsmanship, would provide him with more than suitable transportation for the remainder of his journey. He climbed into his new creation with his provisions in hand and made his way south on the Allegheny River to the recently completed French stronghold, Fort Duquesne, located on the western edge of Pennsylvania.

At Fort Duquesne, the Allegheny River intersected with the Ohio River. Paul steered his canoe to travel west on the Ohio River. His voyage on the river would take him across the entire Ohio Valley for more than six hundred miles until it intersected with the Mississippi River.

About two hundred miles before reaching the Mississippi, Paul spotted choppy waters ahead. He was approaching the Ohio Falls, the only part of the Ohio River considered perilous for navigation. This dangerous section of the Ohio River started with rapids, extending about two miles and descending approximately twenty-six feet, before reaching the actual waterfalls. The Ohio Falls were navigable, but could be treacherous, and in some cases, fatal. However, the Ohio Falls were nothing like the Niagara Falls at the New York and Canadian border where the vertical drop was a staggering one hundred and seventy-six feet. The Ohio Falls dropped only from four to nine feet, depending on the water levels and which side of the river one took.

As Paul entered the rapids two miles before the falls, he saw two fairly large-sized islands dividing the river, creating three chutes in the river. He really had no choice but to take the middle chute since the current was getting too strong for him to steer his canoe toward one side of the river or the other anyway. The current had increased from about a half mile an hour on the river to over ten miles an hour in the rapids.

Paul did not feel as though he was in great danger, but he was a bit apprehensive as to how bad this part of the river might become. He was not so much in fear of drowning as he was afraid of capsizing his canoe and losing his gun, his food, and the rest of his belongings. The rapids were increasing his speed now to about thirteen miles an hour as he descended toward the falls. He was in complete control of the canoe at this point and could see the waterfalls ahead. He had no idea how far the drop might be, but was hoping for the best. As his canoe sped toward the falls, he braced himself as the canoe angled over them. Luckily, Paul hit the falls where the drop was only about four feet. The bow of the canoe crashed down at about a forty-five degree angle, jolting Paul and causing him to lunge forward slightly.  The canoe somehow stayed in a straight line, and more importantly, it stayed afloat.

Paul was relieved he avoided catastrophe.  As he steered his canoe back into calmer waters, he glanced back at the falls, noting that the drop in the falls at the northern and southern parts of the river was probably twice as high as where he passed over in the middle of the river.  He recognized his good fortune at going over the falls at its lowest point.  If he had gone over at just about any other part of the river, he would have lost nearly everything he had, including possibly the canoe and even his life.

When he reached the great Mississippi River, he steered north and rowed for another hundred miles or so until he finally arrived at Kaskaskia.  It had taken him six weeks to get there.  He was thankful to finally arrive at what would be his new home.  It had been a long, strenuous voyage, and he was happy to have made it in one piece.

The town of Kaskaskia was essentially a French village.  It had French-style architecture with rows of low one-story houses lining the streets.  There was only one brick house, built three years prior to Paul's arrival.  The bricks had been brought on a boat all the way across the Ohio River from

Pennsylvania, the same route Paul had just taken. When Paul was later told of the story of the only brick house in town, he was amazed. It must have been a miracle, he thought, that a boat full of bricks managed to go over the Ohio Falls without sinking or losing its cargo.

In the early 1700s, Kaskaskia had consisted of just a few French traders, some of whom had Indian wives. A French priest had settled there with the idea of converting the Indians to Catholicism. A fort was built later on by the French government as the settlement grew. By 1753, Kaskaskia had grown to more than seven hundred people. More and more French settlers from Canada were arriving in Kaskaskia all the time. Many English-speaking people from the Illinois Territory also lived in the settlement. As a result, a majority of the settlers spoke both French and English, including Paul.

Paul was only nineteen years old when he arrived in Kaskaskia in the summer of 1753, but he was mature beyond his youthful years, both in his demeanor and physical appearance. He was dressed in buckskin leggings and a loose-fitting shirt made of animal skin. His clothing was heavily stained with sweat and dirt from his grueling journey on the river. On his belt, he had a hunting knife, a hatchet, a powder horn, and a bullet pouch. He was wearing a wide-brimmed beaver felt hat that had been new when he left Montreal, but now hung tiredly on his head. In his hand, he gripped a long musket as he walked into the settlement.

Scanning the streets as he entered Kaskaskia, Paul was astounded by the number of settlers already living in the town. Farmers near town greeted him with a friendly nod, which he returned. Other people in town merely grunted at him, if they greeted him at all. Most ignored him. Besides being involved in the fur trade, many people in Kaskaskia were farming, while others were mining lead and iron ore on the Missouri side of the river. The mining of this underground wealth was as important to the region's exploration and settlement in the early eighteenth century as the fur trade.

By far the unfriendliest people in town seemed to be the trappers. These men, laden down with furs, were glaring at him, perturbed at the sight of yet another fur trapper in town. The competition was not welcome. The trappers had congregated at the fur trading post, the largest and oldest building in town. The shingle over the door of the building read in French, "La Compagnie du Nord-Ouest," the Northwest Trading Company. The boards out front were warped from the weight of men and pelts.

The air hummed with flies. A blind man could have found the trading post from the smell of sweat alone. Most of the trappers had not bathed in months.

After asking one of the surly trappers where he might find Antoine LeBoeuf, the gruff man grudgingly pointed out the location of Antoine's house up the street. Luckily, Antoine happened to be in town, just back from trading with the Indians on the frontier. After Paul located his cousin, one of the few friendly faces in town, Antoine not only helped him find his own place to live, but he also introduced him to everyone he knew. Antoine proved essential in familiarizing Paul with the fur trading business.

The French operated a fur trading post in Kaskaskia almost since its inception. The fur trade had become a lucrative business. Most of the traders were already dealing with Indians along the Mississippi and Missouri Rivers. Antoine told Paul he would be hard pressed in carving out a niche in the fur trade anywhere near Kaskaskia. Paul had the idea of trading with the Indians back east along the Ohio River in the Ohio Valley where the Shawnee and Delaware tribes were located. Antoine agreed and told Paul he really had no choice but to go to a location that had not already been exploited by the fur traders from Kaskaskia.

Paul would see very little of Antoine again, as both he and his cousin would be constantly crossing the frontier to trade with the Indians in the following years.

# Chapter 2

Paul did not know it, but history was on his side to begin trading with the Shawnee Indians in the Ohio Valley. In the mid-1700s, the powerful Iroquois Confederacy, an alliance of several Native American nations, including the Shawnee and Delaware tribes, dominated a middle ground between the French territory and the British colonies in North America. The French and the English had managed to co-exist peacefully up until this time. The British colonies occupied the eastern coast of America, while the French had claimed lands that covered Canada and the stretch of land following the Mississippi River all the way to Louisiana. In between the French and the British were the Ohio Indian tribes.

The largest of the Ohio Indian tribes, the Shawnee and Delaware, numbered about ten thousand with two thousand warriors. They spread across Ohio with camps along the Miami River, the Little Miami River, and the Sandusky River, as well as into northeastern Ohio and on the banks of the Ohio River. The French and British were competing for trade in the Ohio Valley. The French had managed to get close to the Shawnee Indians some years before through a French fur trader, Pierre Chartier, the son of a French father and Shawnee mother. Pierre

Chartier had succeeded in getting some Shawnee Indians to attack British traders in the 1740s. The British became increasingly worried that the Ohio tribes were aligning with the French. The British urged the Iroquois Tribe to order the Shawnee and the Delaware tribes to return to the Susquehanna Valley, but the Ohio tribes ignored them.

During the King George's War between England and France from 1744 to 1748, a British blockade of Canada stopped the flow of trade goods, causing the French alliance with the Indian tribes to come apart. British traders took advantage of the situation and increased trading throughout the Ohio Valley. To keep the British out, the French needed to find a way to keep their old allies, the Shawnee and Delaware tribes, on their side.

The Iroquois Confederacy signed many treaties with the British, largely unfavorable to the Iroquois and the other tribes they represented, including the Shawnee and the Delaware. First, in the Treaty of Lancaster in 1748, the Iroquois gave away the Shenandoah Valley for a mere two hundred pounds in British sterling. By 1752, the French tried to block British traders from Ohio by building a new line of forts across western Pennsylvania. However, the Iroquois signed the Logstown Treaty in 1752 allowing the British to build a fort in western Pennsylvania.  The British started construction of the fort at a point where the Allegheny and Monongahela Rivers came together to form the Ohio River, the present-day site of Pittsburgh.

The French destroyed the British fort before it was completed and proceeded to build Fort Duquesne at the same location.  A year later, a twenty-one-year-old Virginian, Major George Washington, led British troops to Fort Duquesne to demand that the French abandon their fort there, as well as all of their forts, and to stop building new forts.  The French Commander at Fort Duquesne gave Major Washington a polite refusal.  Major Washington and his troops retreated from Fort Duquesne without any shots being fired from either the British or the French side.

Major Washington's next expedition to Fort Duquesne in 1754 resulted in a fight killing ten French soldiers without taking the fort, marking the beginning of the French and Indian War that would last until 1763.  The Ohio Indian tribes had been ready to join the side of the British until learning that the Iroquois had ceded Ohio to the British at the Albany Conference.  The Albany Conference took place in May 1754 in Albany, New York, between Iroquois leaders and British representatives sent by the legislatures of the northern seven of the thirteen British colonies.

The Ohio tribes stayed neutral in the French and Indian War until the summer of 1755. In July 1755, General Edward Braddock led a British army of two thousand and one hundred men to attack Fort Duquesne yet again. George Washington, now a Colonel, was one of his officers. Before reaching the fort, General Braddock and his army were ambushed by the French and Indians near the Monongahela River. Colonel Washington had tried to warn General Braddock regarding his tactics in the battle. The French soldiers, and especially their Indian allies, did not fight out in the open in formation as the British fought. The far smaller French and Indian forces opened fire on the British army in a surprise attack from their concealment in the trees.

On that fateful day of July 9, 1755, just south of Fort Duquesne along the Monongahela River, a long line of British soldiers and militia marched toward Fort Duquesne, led by General Braddock on horseback. Colonel Washington rode behind him. Fort Duquesne was only a few miles in the distance.

"Colonel Washington, have the men fall into formation to march on Fort Duquesne," General Braddock said.

"Yes sir," Colonel Washington responded.

As General Braddock pointed to a long meadow with trees lining both sides, he ordered, "Take the men through here."

"General Braddock, marching the men out in the open may not be a good idea, sir," Colonel Washington said.

General Braddock, visibly annoyed, said, "Colonel Washington, don't be insolent...send the men forward."

"With all due respect, General, this approach could prove fatal," Colonel Washington continued. "The French troops, and particularly the Indians, may not be fighting us out in the open."

"Colonel Washington, you are a good, brave soldier, but leave the tactics of fighting to me. After all, you have failed twice already in taking this fort," General Braddock said to him disparagingly.

Colonel Washington knew his instincts were right, but he was in no position to argue with the General. Colonel Washington, ever the dutiful soldier, signaled to the troops to move forward, raising his arm in the air. He dropped his arm forcefully and commanded, "Troops, march."

His subordinate officers repeated the order several times down the line to the British troops.

The British troops moved into rank and file formation marching into the meadow. The French and Indians were hiding in the trees on each side poised to shoot at the approaching British troops.

A French Officer readied his troops with his instructions, "Attendez mon ordre."

The British troops and militia continued through the meadow in ranks about a quarter of a mile long.

The French Officer in the trees gave the command to shoot, yelling, "Tirez!"

The French soldiers and their Indian allies fired their muskets simultaneously from one large section of the woods, fully unanticipated by the British army, except of course, by Colonel Washington. British troops immediately fell to the ground, many groaning in pain at the impact of the musket balls.

Another French Officer yelled, "Tirez!"

Many more French and Indians discharged their weapons from another section of the woods. More British troops plummeted to the ground, lying in the grass either in agony or dead.

Yet another French Officer ordered, "Tirez!"

The French and Indians fired more shots, and more British troops collapsed.  The dead and wounded British soldiers were piling up on one another.

"Tirez!" shouted another French Officer.

British troops were dying en masse.

The French and Indians continued shooting from the trees, hidden and well protected from their enemy.  The gallant British troops attempted to keep in formation and fire back, but nonetheless continued to be slaughtered. They fought valiantly, but to no avail.  The British troops in the front formations began to fall back while the rear units continued advancing in the smoke and confusion of the battle.  The British soldiers became increasingly disoriented and disorganized at not seeing the enemy.  Colonel Washington, still on horseback, motioned to his troops, desperately issuing orders trying to organize them in the futile battle.

"Fall into formation men," he cried.

Colonel Washington fired his weapon from

his horse at the enemy as bullets pierced through his jacket just missing his flesh, leaving gaping holes in his uniform. Colonel Washington, as always, proved to be the bravest and most fearless soldier in the heat of battle, unaffected by the sound of gunshots popping all around him, but the situation was hopeless. The British troops managed to shoot and kill some of their enemy, but very few casualties were inflicted upon the French and Indians. The battle was a total rout of the British army.

British troops continued being shot unmercifully. Even General Braddock was shot off his horse. Colonel Washington was on horseback near General Braddock when the General fell in battle. Colonel Washington could see the day was lost. Taking command, Colonel Washington gave orders to his soldiers, "Fall back, men. Retreat!"

The British army retreated back toward the river leaving a trail of hundreds of dead and wounded men in the meadow. Colonel Washington climbed off his horse to aid the mortally wounded General Braddock. Colonel Washington waved to a soldier in the immediate vicinity for assistance.

"Help me with the General, private," Colonel Washington said.

Colonel Washington put his arm underneath General Braddock's neck.  The private helped him lift General Braddock onto Colonel Washington's horse.  Colonel Washington rode General Braddock away from the battlefield to safety by the Monongahela River.  He motioned to another soldier by the river tending to the wounded.  The soldier helped Colonel Washington lift General Braddock off the horse and they lowered him gently to the ground.  Colonel Washington knelt down next to General Braddock.

"The men fought bravely," General Braddock said to Colonel Washington in a weak, dying, faint voice.  "I am proud of them."

General Braddock's head wilted sideways as he died.  Colonel Washington bowed his head in sorrow.  He not only felt deep regret for General Braddock's death, but also for all of the other brave men who perished.  Colonel Washington would be writing hundreds of sad letters to the families of the slain soldiers, a duty he dreaded after every battle.  He also knew the wounded were in serious trouble.  Wounds to the gut of a soldier often meant a slow, painful death.  Bullet wounds to limbs frequently required crude amputations.  Most of the soldiers treated for their injuries had a high probability of suffering and dying from infections later.  Many of the brave, injured

soldiers who had fallen would likely never fight
again.  It was a sad day all around.

In the end, almost five hundred British
soldiers were killed and another four hundred
were wounded.  Casualties for the French and
Indians were a mere eight French troops killed,
fifteen Indians killed, and only a total of
fifteen more combined French and Indians
wounded.

Two days later, when the news of this
horrible massacre reached the British colonies
back east, disbelief was followed by vehement
anger, especially toward native Indians.
Although the Shawnee and Delaware warriors had
no participation in the battle, they had chosen
an inopportune time to send a delegation to
Philadelphia to protest the Iroquois cession of
Ohio to the British, negotiated the year before
at the Albany Conference.

On July 11, 1755 in Philadelphia,
Pennsylvania, a delegation of two Shawnee
Indians and one Delaware Indian arrived in the
city.  They slowly rode on horseback through the
busy Philadelphia streets to make their protest
to the British at the recently completed
Pennsylvania State House, which later became
more famously known as Independence Hall during
the American Revolution.  Nearly every person on
the city streets stopped and stared at them.  It

was not every day Indians were seen riding down the streets of Philadelphia. Most city dwellers had never seen Indians in the flesh. They had heard stories, read about them in newspapers, and even seen illustrations in books, but most had never seen an actual Indian. A large crowd gathered across the street from the Pennsylvania State House as the Indians entered the building. The three Indians sat at a long table directly across from the British Deputy Governor of Pennsylvania, Robert Hunter Morris, and his three British advisors.

The Shawnee Indian acting as the spokesman for the Indians addressed the British delegation in English. "We have come to protest the Iroquois speaking on our behalf," the Indian said. "The Iroquois cannot give up land that is not theirs to give. The Shawnee and the Delaware tribes are not giving up their lands in Ohio to the English."

As the British delegation was intently listening, they heard noise and commotion from the streets. Morris went to the window to see the crowd gathering outside. He opened the window and asked a man in the street, "What's happening?"

"General Braddock was killed two days ago at Fort Duquesne by the French and the Injuns," the man in the street said in an excited and loud voice. "They're sayin' over a thousand Braddock boys are dead and wounded!"

"God help us," Morris said, astonished by this news.

"They were probably there," the man outside bellowed angrily, pointing through the window to the Indians inside. "The Injuns done it."

"Get the soldiers and bring them here," Morris said in a subdued voice. The man outside ran up the street to find soldiers. Morris turned around from the window, now directing his comments to the Indians at the table.

"You murderers dare to come here and make demands of us," he said in a most condemning voice.

The Indian who had spoken previously had a puzzled look on his face. He looked side to side at the Indians seated next to him, wondering what had happened. The other two Indians were perplexed as well. The Indian looked back at Morris and said incredulously, "We know of no such battle."

"I doubt that," Morris said.

A few minutes later, British soldiers entered the room.

"Arrest these Indians," Morris ordered. The soldiers seized the three Indians. They were jailed and hanged three days later by order of Deputy Governor Morris. Their executions were carried out simply as revenge and hatred for Indians at large. The three Indians were entirely innocent, but received no trial or any type of formal hearing. They had personally taken no part in the fighting at Fort Duquesne. In fact, no Shawnee or Delaware warriors whatsoever took part in the battle at Fort Duquesne. The Shawnee and Delaware Indian tribes had not fought on the side of the French against the British army at any time up to that point in the war.

When the members of the Shawnee and Delaware tribes in the Ohio Valley learned of the horrific act committed against their Indian brothers in Philadelphia, they were incensed beyond any form of comprehension. There would be no question as to whose side they would take in the war now. The Shawnee and Delaware were categorically against the British for unjustly executing their three innocent tribe members. They were not necessarily fighting on the French side, although this was the unintended consequence, as much as they were at that moment undeniably against the British for their unfair and prejudicial actions. After the news of the hangings reached the Ohio tribes, Shawnee and

Delaware war parties began attacking British settlements on the frontiers of Pennsylvania, Maryland, and Virginia, savagely killing more than two thousand and five hundred colonists during the next two years.

When Paul began his career as a fur trader, he had no idea of the overwhelming effect any of these historical events would have on his personal life and future. In 1753, he merely viewed going into the Ohio Valley as a matter of necessity for economic reasons. The fur traders from Kaskaskia already had a monopoly on trading with the Indians in the Illinois Territory and areas west of the Mississippi River. Few fur traders ventured back east to the Ohio Valley. It became evident to Paul that his success depended upon exploring an area where less competition existed. Paul believed his chances of gaining a stronghold with an Ohio Indian tribe would be better than with a tribe out west.

After deciding on the Ohio Valley as his destination, Paul's first order of business was to improve the condition of his canoe he had so hastily made the month before. The crude canoe he carved out from the birch tree in the Allegheny Mountains on his way to Kaskaskia had not provided him with the most comfortable ride. With the assistance of his cousin, Antoine, Paul was able to obtain some proper sanding tools. He worked meticulously on smoothing out the wood in the interior and exterior of his canoe. By the time he was through, the finish was so polished and smooth, a man could have run his hand over every inch of it without getting even a trace of a splinter.

Before long, Paul was eager to load his freshly refurbished canoe with trading goods and make his way south nearly a hundred miles down the Mississippi River to the Ohio River. He paddled east about two hundred miles on the Ohio. When he heard the Ohio Falls thundering in the distance, he knew it would soon be time to head toward shore. The only way around the falls and the rapids would be to drag his canoe along the edge of the river. The canoe was fairly lightweight on its own, but it was loaded down with supplies and trading goods. He managed to drag it around the falls and pull it another two miles downriver beyond the rapids. It took Paul hours to finally arrive at a location where he could safely get back on the river to resume his journey.

Due to his severe exhaustion, he decided to camp for the night before continuing downriver. It was close to dusk anyway. He rarely ever traveled the river at night. In the morning, after finishing his coffee and eating rabbit for breakfast, he extinguished his campfire and pushed his canoe back onto the river.  Over the next six days, he traveled east on the Ohio River for more than one hundred and fifty miles and north on the Little Miami River for another fifty miles, a trip he would make numerous times during the next three years.  He had forged a bond with the Shawnee Indians, more specifically with their leader, Chief Black Hoof.  Their tribe was encamped near the Little Miami River, not far from the present-day town of Xenia, Ohio.  However, no white men lived there then, only Indians inhabited this area of the Ohio Valley during the mid-1700s.

# Chapter 3

From 1753 to 1755, Paul made numerous successful trips from Kaskaskia to the Shawnee Indian camp. On his latest voyage in early July 1755, Paul again rowed his canoe filled with trading goods to the shore on the Little Miami River to trade with the Shawnee. He unloaded all types of merchandise, including iron axes, knives, blankets, brass kettles, jewelry, and even three small barrels of rum. Paul pulled the canoe onto the riverbank and covered it up with brush. He heaved his packs of goods over each shoulder and began walking into the woods toward the camp.

As Paul walked out of the trees near the edge of the Shawnee Indian camp, he saw Chief Black Hoof in front of his tent conversing with other Indians in the tribe. Paul laid down his large packs of goods and strode toward Chief Black Hoof. As Chief Black Hoof turned to greet Paul, his face lit up with joy, obviously pleased to see him again.

Chief Black Hoof, speaking in his Shawnee language, said jubilantly, "Larsh, you have returned."

Chief Black Hoof always referred to Paul as Larsh, rather than his full name, L'Archevêque. The shorter name flowed off his tongue much

easier.  L'Archevêque was a mouthful not only
for the Shawnee, but for any man.

"Yes, Chief Black Hoof," Paul said, also
speaking Shawnee.  "I have traveled many miles
down many long rivers to bring you axes, knives,
blankets, and rum."

Paul spoke the Shawnee language fluently as
a result of his frequent visits trading with the
Indians.  Although Chief Black Hoof knew both a
little bit of French and some English, the two
conversed exclusively in Shawnee.

"These things are useful to us, Larsh,"
Chief Black Hoof said.  "Come into my tent.  We
must talk."  The two friends entered the Chief's
tent alone.

"The white men are fighting," Chief Black
Hoof said to Paul, his expression having now
changed from one of delight to absolute
seriousness.  "Your people are fighting the
English and building forts at the edge of our
land.  The Iroquois have made many treaties with
the English, but they do not represent us.  The
Iroquois have given our land to the English, but
it is not theirs to give.  I have sent two
Shawnee representatives, accompanied by a
Delaware tribe representative, to talk with the
English in the east to tell them that their
people cannot come to our land to live.  Indians

from many tribes have already gone east to help your people fight the English. I will not take sides in this war if I can help it. I will wait to see if the English will honor our wishes and listen to the Shawnee."

"I know nothing of this war," Paul responded. "I am a simple trader who only wishes to continue our business together as friends."

"You are a good and honest man, Larsh," Chief Black Hoof said to Paul. "I hope not to go to war with your people or the English. My only wish is for the Shawnee to hunt and fish on our own lands with no white settlers interfering."

Weeks later, Paul arrived back at the dock on the Mississippi River at the Kaskaskia settlement. Paul unloaded a sizeable stack of beaver and mink pelts onto the dock. Paul headed into town with his pelts flung over his shoulder to the Northwest Trading Company.

As he entered the trading post, he greeted the clerk, "Bonsoir, Pierre. How are you?"

"I am well, Paul," Pierre said. "We were worried about you. You have been gone so long."

"I had a good trip," Paul told him. "I believe the Shawnee now trust me completely. I hope to be bringing back many more pelts for a long time to come."

As Paul laid his large stack of beaver and mink pelts on the counter, Pierre inspected them while writing figures on a piece of paper.

"You have twenty-four minks at five livres and ten sols per pelt," Pierre said. "I count thirty-seven beaver pelts at six livres and ten sols each. That's a total of three hundred and seventy-two livres and ten sols."

Pierre handed Paul fifteen French gold coins worth twenty-four livres each, twelve French one-livre silver coins, and ten French sols in silver coins.

"Just be careful, my friend," Pierre said. "Don't let those redskins scalp those long wavy locks of yours."

Paul put the gold and silver coins in his pocket, smiled and said, "Bonsoir, Pierre" as he departed.

"Bonsoir," Pierre said, waving and smiling back at Paul.

As Paul exited the trading post, he ran into his good friend, Guillaume Hennet, the owner of the General Store, who was walking down the street toward him.

"Guillaume," Paul said as he shook hands with him as they met. "I am so happy to see you again."

"Paul, my friend, you are back safely," Guillaume said. "I am so glad."

"Of course I am, why wouldn't I?" Paul responded with self-confidence.

"News has reached us that the French and Indians massacred British troops outside of Fort Duquesne," Guillaume said as his voice changed to a very somber tone. "A trader from Fort Duquesne arrived yesterday. He said Shawnee war parties are raiding English settlements all over Pennsylvania, Maryland, and Virginia."

"What?" Paul said. "I just spoke with Chief Black Hoof a few weeks ago. He said he did not want to take sides."

"It was most unfortunate for the Shawnee and Delaware Indians who happened to be in Philadelphia at the time of the attack," Guillaume said.

"Why? What happened?" Paul asked. "Chief Black Hoof told me he was sending Shawnee representatives to protest the Iroquois treaty with the English."

"The English hanged them immediately,"

Guillaume told him.

"You must be joking," Paul said in total surprise. "I know Chief Black Hoof. He will be out for revenge for this despicable act. He'll hate the English with a passion. The Shawnee were not exactly with the French in this war, but they will definitely be against the English now."

"You cannot go back there to trade," Guillaume said worriedly. "It is far too dangerous. The Indians are already getting their revenge murdering settlers."

"I will be all right," Paul said, trying to reassure him. "At the moment, they hate the English, not the French. Besides, I am making far too much money. I'll be at your store soon enough to load up for another trip."

Paul left Guillaume and entered his small one-room house down the street. The house had a fireplace, a table and chair on one side of the room, and a bed and dresser on the other side. Paul pushed the dresser aside and pulled up a floorboard. Below the floorboard, he dug down in the dirt pulling out a wooden box filled with French money. He removed the gold and silver coins from his pocket he received from Pierre earlier and placed them into the box. Paul closed up the box and buried it back into the dirt.  He carefully placed the floorboard back and pushed the dresser over top.  Afterward, he jumped into bed to sleep with dreams of a growing fortune.

# Chapter 4

At dusk on a calm autumn evening in late September 1756, a band of raiding Shawnee Indian warriors rode on horseback over the Shenandoah Mountains. Below the mountains, farmhouses dotted the countryside near and around the town of Jackson River in Augusta County, Virginia, in the scenic Shenandoah Valley. One of the farmhouses was the home of George and Alice Kincaid. The Kincaids had three children, William, David, and Mary, age nine, six, and four months old, respectively. George Kincaid was born in Scotland in 1720. He immigrated to America arriving on a ship to New York in 1746. He married Alice Dean that same year when she was just sixteen years old. She was the daughter of William Dean and Sarah Campbell of New York.

George and Alice Kincaid moved to the James River settlement in Augusta County, Virginia, after their marriage. George had an uncle there, David Kincaid, who had emigrated from Scotland to Virginia in 1715. David Kincaid was the brother of the Laird of the Kincaid Clan in Scotland and had taken part in the Stuart Rebellion of 1715. After the failed rebellion, David Kincaid fled Scotland. He was one of the first settlers in the Shenandoah Valley and reared a large family. He built the first

Augusta County jail. George and Alice were very happy on their farm with their three children in this beautiful countryside. It was seemingly an idyllic place to raise a family, at least until that late September evening in 1756.

On the night of the raid by the Shawnee warriors, George was pumping water into a bucket in front of his small farmhouse. George's bright orange hair, typical of many Scotsmen, was shining in the moonlight. He walked through the front door of the house with the bucket of water. His pretty young wife, Alice, was seated in a rocking chair by the fireplace reading her beloved King James Bible, a wedding present from her mother. Her baby girl, Mary, was in the crib next to her. Her two small boys, William and David, were playing with their wooden toy blocks, stacking them as high as they could and then watching them teeter and fall. They happily repeated this game over and over again. It was a typical evening in the Kincaid home. Everyone was relaxing as they prepared for bed. William was not yet in his pajamas, but was still dressed in his favorite blue hunting jacket. David had already changed into his bedclothes.

"All right, boys, I've got some water," George said in his thick Scottish brogue as he entered the house. "Wash your face and hands and get ready for bed."

"Aaawww, Papa, do we have to?" the boys pled in unison.

"George, keep the door open so we can get the evening breeze," Alice said. "'Tis been so hot today."

George put down the pail of water and turned to open the front door he had just closed. As he opened the door, his eyes got big as he saw Indians fast approaching on horseback. Before he could even react, an arrow pierced right through his heart.

George winced in agony, moaning "Aaahhh!" before he slowly fell over onto the front porch from his mortal wound. Alice spontaneously jumped up out of her rocking chair, still holding the Bible she was reading. After seeing George's limp dead body, she instinctively turned to grab and protect her baby. She put her Bible safely in the pocket of her dress as she picked up Mary from the cradle. Alice held the baby as tightly as she had ever held any child in her life, terrified of the unfolding situation. She looked on helplessly at her two boys. William and David were dumbfounded, not quite sure what was happening.

The raiding Indians shot several burning

arrows with great precision from the backs of their racing horses, each hitting the walls of the farmhouse and more landing on the rooftop, causing a conflagration in each area hit. The farmhouse quickly became engulfed in flames with smoke thickening inside. Clutching Mary in her arms, Alice ran from the fiery house coughing, trying desperately to breathe some fresh air into her lungs. William and David followed her to escape the inferno. One of the raiding Indians snatched up David onto his horse at a full gallop while another powerful Indian grabbed William, hurling him in an instant onto the back of his horse. Alice stood defenselessly outside her burning home with her baby, intensely disturbed by the mayhem going on around her.

Alice watched in horror as a crazed Indian darted to George's motionless body lying in the doorway of the house. The Indian grabbed a hold of George's hair and proceeded to gruesomely scalp him with a very large knife. The savage Indian turned to his fellow raiders and held up George's orange-haired scalp into the air triumphantly, blood running down the Indian's out-stretched arm. George's lifeless body now lay on the porch with his mutilated head in a puddle of blood, the flames and smoke shooting out of the front door of the hellhole that was once their home. Alice was stunned at the ghastly sight of her dead husband. The Indians continued their rampage slinging more burning arrows into the barn next to the farmhouse.

An Indian on horseback approached Alice, who was now standing over her disfigured husband. She was dangerously close to the sweltering fiery house. The Indian motioned for her to climb aboard his horse. Alice did not move, but just stood there, cuddling and shielding her baby. The Indian jumped off his horse, grasped her under her arm, and hoisted her and the baby onto the horse. He leaped back on, energetically riding Alice and her daughter away from the horrendous scene of their devastated home. The remainder of the marauding Indians followed. The farmhouse and barn burned to the ground.

Shawnee and Delaware war parties from other encampments in Ohio had attacked several additional homesteads around Jackson River in Augusta County that evening, killing a total of fourteen men, women, and children, and taking a dozen more prisoners back to their respective camps.

The band of Shawnee Indians with Alice and her three children as their prisoners headed west up the Shenandoah Mountains, oblivious to the carnage they left behind. From the back of the horse she was riding, Alice turned for a view of the valley. She was already distraught, but became further distressed after seeing dozens of homes in flames in the town and throughout the countryside. She realized then that many of her friends and relatives in the settlement probably met the same fate as George and the rest of her family. They were perhaps dead or prisoners too. Alice hung her head as tears ran down her face, consumed with feelings of misery and bewilderment. David cried uncontrollably as they continued over the mountain. William was solemn, but more subdued, never once crying or making a sound. Alice did not know it yet, but she and her children were being taken more than two hundred miles to Shawnee Chief Black Hoof's Indian camp on the Little Miami River in the Ohio Valley.

The next day, the Indians slowly made their way on horseback through the mountains toward their destination. David continued crying incessantly, still seated on the back of one of the horses an Indian was riding. Another Indian on horseback became agitated at David's endless weeping.

The Indian, speaking in the Shawnee language, shouted furiously to David, "Be quiet young one or I will hit you with this club."

David had no idea what he said. Neither Alice nor William knew either. The irate Indian only made David cry louder. The Indian inexplicably hit David with his club, knocking the defenseless child off the horse. David fell six feet to the ground, hitting his head on a large sharp rock. David lay still on the ground, his head coming to rest in a pool of bright red blood. David's crying had eerily stopped. The poor harmless boy was dead.

The Indian who had just killed David showed no remorse, only rage. Alice watched in terror, too afraid to scream. Tears rolled down her cheeks as she glared at the Indian who had just brutally killed her son. Her face revealed deep anguish at the Indian's horrific actions. Alice noticed George's bright orange scalp hanging on the Indian's belt. She knew not to make a sound to avoid this cruel and ruthless Indian from taking his irritation out on her. She cuddled her baby in her arms tightly and quickly averted her eyes from the deranged Indian. The abject fear and unfathomable torment Alice felt was almost more than she could bear.

"Oh, please dear Lord, help us," Alice whispered, praying to her herself.

Days later during the evening, the Indians arrived at the Shawnee Indian camp near the Little Miami River. At the edge of camp, the remaining members of the Kincaid family climbed down off the backs of the horses they had been riding. The Indian warriors, including the warrior with George's scalp on his belt, shoved them toward the center of the camp. William was still dressed in his blue hunting jacket. Alice was clutching Mary tightly to her bosom. The Kincaids were pushed in front of Chief Black Hoof near his tent. The entire tribe was gathered around.

Alice grasped hold of her Bible in the pocket of her dress and recited a prayer as she awaited her fate. She whispered a passage from the Bible she knew by heart, the twenty-third Psalm, "The Lord is my shepherd; I shall not want. He maketh me to lie down in green pastures: he leadeth me beside the still waters. He restoreth my soul: he leadeth me in the path of righteousness for his name's sake. Yea, though I walk through the valley of the shadow of death, I will fear no evil: for thou art with me; thy rod and thy staff they comfort me. Thou preparest a table before me in the presence of mine enemies: thou anointest my head with oil; my cup runneth over. Surely goodness and mercy shall follow me all the days of my life: and I will dwell in the house of the Lord forever."

At the other end of camp, some one hundred yards or so away, stood Paul. He had arrived earlier in the day and was preparing for trading

46

with the Shawnee. He watched intently as the prisoners were brought into camp and presented to Chief Black Hoof. Paul's interest in the ongoing happenings went unnoticed by the preoccupied Indians. Paul calmly filled his pipe with tobacco and smoked it. His eyes were fixed on the activities in camp, curious as to how events would unfold.

The Indian with George's scalp addressed Chief Black Hoof. Speaking in Shawnee, which only Paul and the Indians understood, the Indian said, "Our war party and the other Shawnee war parties, as well as the other invading Indian nations, have destroyed the English settlement in the Shenandoah Valley, Great Chief. We bring you back prisoners."

"You have done well," Chief Black Hoof said. "The English will fear us and keep far from us."

Chief Black Hoof stared into Alice's eyes. He felt an immediate attraction, as probably any normal man would, no matter whether he was a white man or an Indian. After all, she was a very alluring, dark-haired, well-built, young woman. Despite the tragedy that had just befallen her, and the rather grim circumstances awaiting her and the remainder of her family, she still projected the appearance of an exceptionally striking woman. Chief Black Hoof could appreciate her beauty even as she was experiencing her darkest moments of despair. Chief Black Hoof took hold of Alice's arm and turned her toward the tribe announcing, "I will take this white woman as my squaw."

The Indians in the tribe yelled and cheered, waving their arms in the air, reveling in both their victory and the Chief's announcement. Chief Black Hoof pulled Alice and her baby into his tent. Chief Black Hoof ogled Alice, grinning all the while, obviously satisfied with his new squaw. Alice was thinner than most of the squaws in camp, but she wasn't scrawny. Alice glared back at Chief Black Hoof and spat in his face. She made it perfectly clear to him she was repulsed to be in his presence. Alice would rather be dead than be with the man whom she regarded as responsible for the deaths of her husband and son.

Chief Black Hoof became infuriated. He was humiliated by her actions. Alice could see in the Chief's face that he wanted to kill her. Alice's expression quickly turned from defiance to fear. Chief Black Hoof could not tolerate this rejection. She had insulted his position as Chief and bruised his ego. Chief Black Hoof forced her out the opening of the tent, still holding her arm firmly as they exited. He was seething. He pushed her and the baby forward into the grasp of the Indian with George's scalp.

"Run them through the gauntlet," the Chief said angrily. "And the boy, too."

Although she had not understood a word of Shawnee, Alice knew Chief Black Hoof was enraged. Outright terror came over her as she came to the realization of what was about to happen. The Indian with her husband's scalp signaled to the others to prepare the gauntlet. The Indians picked up clubs, sticks, and whips, and formed two lines down the middle of camp, approximately thirty to forty Indians on each side. Alice was pushed to the start of the gauntlet. She was clutching her baby much more firmly to shield her from harm, anticipating the violence about to be inflicted upon them.

The Indian shoved her forcibly in between the two lines, but she moved very slowly at first, not wanting to run toward a beating. As the Indians on each side of the line screamed and danced, they hit her repeatedly with their sticks, clubs, and whips. Alice began to gradually speed up, as her instinct now was to run away from the battering. However, there was no getting away. As she was hit about the face and head, she raised her left arm up in order to protect her face. She was now holding the baby with only her right arm. The baby was also getting hit in the head as she propelled herself forward through the gauntlet, desperately trying to move past the vicious Indians.

William looked on with abhorrence as his mother and baby sister were being struck continuously. An Indian was holding William tightly at the front of the gauntlet, waiting for his turn. William's entire body tensed up like an untamed animal about to be unleashed. William was teary-eyed and anguished, but he was not openly crying. He wanted to defend his mother and sister in the worst way, but he was powerless to do anything. Alice finally reached the end of the gauntlet, but after having been struck repeatedly, she fell unconscious dropping her baby. The baby lay motionless on the ground beside her, lifeless.

The Indians continued with their howls and screams, obviously enjoying this ritual and the sheer brutality of it. William was next in line to run the gauntlet. He understandably remained tremendously upset, but the expression on his face revealed more of the defiance he felt. As the Indian holding William pushed him to run the gauntlet, the Indians began hitting him fiercely. Surprisingly, William returned the blows with his fists, swinging his arms wildly. Although the Indians struck him in the head and face numerous times, many of the blows drawing blood, William continued to fight back with a vengeance. Despite his very young age, William displayed great courage. He was not going down without a fight. His actions greatly pleased Chief Black Hoof.

Chief Black Hoof called out to his tribe members on the gauntlet line, "Stop! Stop! Do not hurt the boy!"

The two rows of Indians on the gauntlet line immediately ceased beating on William. William was stupefied. He presumed he was going to be beaten to death.

Chief Black Hoof walked toward the puzzled boy, visibly impressed with his boldness, bravery, and courage. Chief Black Hoof stated to the tribe, "This boy has great worth. He will make a fine warrior." Chief Black Hoof held William affectionately by the shoulders. William's heart was racing, but he quickly began to calm down as he realized his punishment would not continue.

"We will call him 'Blue Jacket'," Chief Black Hoof pronounced to the tribe.

The wild Indians cheered and continued yelling in spirited celebration as they broke up the two lines of the gauntlet. Alice still lay on the ground unconscious, her baby dead, while the Indians continued celebrating as if she and her baby were not even there. William was relieved when it became apparent to him he was being spared. However, he was pained to see his mother and sister lying on the ground, believing both were dead.

Paul continued watching the events from a short distance away just outside camp. He calmly continued smoking his pipe while observing the raucous activity of the Indians. As he finished smoking, he cleaned his pipe out by knocking it against a tree. He retired to his tent pondering the atrocity he had just witnessed.

The next morning, Paul gathered some sticks to make a fire to boil water in a kettle for his morning coffee. Paul surveyed the landscape in the Indian camp that revealed many Indians out and about working in their normal daily activities, a stark contrast to the pandemonium from the previous night. Paul began organizing his goods to take into the camp for trading. He stopped momentarily to drink his cup of coffee and continued his preparation for the day's trading. After assembling his trade goods, Paul carried them to an area outside Chief Black Hoof's tent where their transactions normally took place.

Upon seeing Paul approach, Chief Black Hoof

invited him to sit on a large blanket with the other Indians present. Paul methodically spread out his goods on the blanket. His first order of business was trading metal plates. With a stack of plates in front of him, Paul held up his hand with two fingers to Chief Black Hoof, indicating he wanted two beaver pelts for the plates. Chief Black Hoof nodded in agreement. Another Indian took the plates and handed Paul his two pelts.

This trading continued for hours with other goods being offered such as brass kettles, iron axes, knives, blankets, jewelry, and barrels of rum. Each transaction concluded with the Chief either nodding in approval or shaking his head with dissatisfaction. Paul finished the trading after all of his goods were gone with a firm handshake with Chief Black Hoof. Both Chief Black Hoof and Paul were pleased with the outcome of the exchanges. Paul picked up his large number of beaver and mink pelts, hoisting them on his back, and departed to his tent at the edge of camp.

Paul spotted Alice outside camp picking up sticks as he made his way back to his tent. Paul was quite surprised at seeing her. After witnessing her run the gauntlet the night before and falling unconscious at the end of it, he had assumed she was dead. The Indian with George's

scalp saw Paul looking at Alice. The Indian
said to Paul in Shawnee, "The white woman is
making preparations for her fate tonight," as he
eyed the stake in the center of the camp.

Paul looked to the center of camp and saw
the six-foot high wooden pole, immediately
realizing Alice's impending doom.

"I thought she had been killed last night,"
Paul said. "What became of her baby?"

"Baby dead," the Indian responded.

"That's a shame," Paul said flippantly.
"Now you won't be able to burn the baby at the
stake, too."

The Indian with George's scalp did not
recognize Paul's sarcasm and merely walked back
into the camp. Paul continued toward his tent
with his pelts piled high in his arms. He
watched Alice as she picked up sticks, bundling
them in her arms. Alice was moving ever so
slowly and appeared to be in a daze. Paul
finally made eye contact with Alice. She was
bruised and cut about the face. Paul motioned
with his head for her to make her way toward his
tent, his arms still full. She obliged, limping
and moving ever so carefully, obviously in pain
from her flogging. Paul arrived at his tent and
began organizing his pelts and goods. He

glanced back at camp making sure no Indians were watching. Alice came nearer to the tent looking weak and confused.

"Do you have any idea what's about to happen to you?" he whispered to Alice.

Alice shook her head, indicating no.

"You are gatherin' sticks for your own death," he told her.

"What do you mean?" she replied.

"They are goin' to kill you," he said. "You are goin' to be burned at the stake tonight."

"I can't bear any more of this nightmare," she said, as a look of dread crossed her face.

Alice's body wilted and she appeared as if she might collapse to the ground. Paul grabbed her around the waist to give her support so she did not fall. He again looked toward the Indian camp to make sure no one had seen them. He was very nervous they might be seen together. Paul was astutely aware of the Shawnee prohibition of any outsider interfering in their business. Paul was treading on very thin ice just speaking with Alice, let alone physically assisting her.

"You need to collect yourself," he told

her.  "I might be able to get you away from here."

"I'm too weary to run away," Alice said.

"Don't worry," Paul quickly responded. "I'll carry you out if you're too weak."

"I can't leave my son behind," Alice said. "He's all I have left."

"I can't get you both out," Paul explained. "They're keepin' your son on the other side of the camp.  I don't know which tent he's in.  If we're caught, they'll kill us all."

"Then I won't go," Alice boldly said.

"If you stay, your son will see you burned at the stake tonight," Paul pleaded.  "That's not something you want.  I personally don't need to see it.  You definitely don't want your boy witnessin' that.  If you leave with me tonight, he'll be safe."

Alice stared straight ahead, as if in a trance, in deep thought reconsidering Paul's offer.

"The Shawnee won't harm him," Paul continued.  "It's clear they want to adopt him. The Shawnee value the worth of a person.  They don't care about the color of somebody's skin.

They only see the content of that person. That's all that matters to them."

"Is this why they let you trade with 'em?" Alice asked.

"Maybe, but the point is, your boy's bein' adopted by the Shawnee no matter what, whether you die or don't die," Paul answered. "If you stay, you'll be burned at the stake just as sure as we're standin' here. And your son's goin' to have to suffer, too, by watchin' you die in agony."

Alice's eyes suddenly opened very wide. She finally grasped the meaning of what Paul had been so patiently trying to explain to her. She realized that Paul was absolutely right. She could not allow her son to witness his own mother being burned alive.

"If you let me take you away from here, you can spare him this pain," Paul further clarified. "Either way, the Shawnee won't hurt him."

"All right, I'll go," Alice finally said.

"Good," Paul said resolutely. "I'll watch you when you go back to camp to see the tent where they're keepin' you. I'll come for you just after sunset."

Paul checked back in camp yet again, making sure none of the Indians had seen them talking together.  Alice slowly walked back toward her tent with her bundle of sticks.  Paul took note of the tent she entered.

Later on, just before sunset, Paul removed all of his belongings from his tent, including his pelts from the trading earlier in the day, and carried them through the woods to load them into his canoe by the river.

That night, Paul snuck up to the edge of camp and watched the tent where they were keeping Alice.  He surveyed the Indians congregating at the center of camp where the stake was located.  A large pile of brush and sticks was at its base.  Paul spotted a squaw leaving the tent where Alice was being kept.  He crept up to the tent, snuck inside, and found Alice lying on a blanket, her Bible next to her.

Alice was awake but told Paul, "I am so exhausted.  I can't do it."

"Don't worry," Paul reassured her.  "I'll carry you.  Just stay quiet."

"My Bible!" Alice cried.

"Here it is," Paul said, picking it up off the blanket and handing it to her.

Alice carefully placed the Bible in the pocket of her tattered gingham dress. Paul easily picked up Alice in her blanket. Alice was not a large woman. She was petite in size, but sturdy and well-proportioned. He turned toward the opening of the tent and paused before checking to see if it was safe to exit. He quickly darted out with Alice bundled in his arms. No Indians were nearby so he ran from camp like a frightened deer being hunted. He sprinted past his own tent and disappeared into the trees.

Moments later, the squaw returned and looked inside Alice's tent. After seeing no sign of Alice, the squaw rushed out excitedly, racing back to the center of camp to Chief Black Hoof and the tribe of Indians to inform them that the white woman was gone.

Visibly annoyed, Chief Black Hoof ordered, "Check the camp and find her."

The Indians scattered and began searching each tent in the camp. Meanwhile, Paul dashed out of the woods and laid Alice down on the riverbank. He pulled the brush off his canoe and dragged it into the shallow water.

The Indians searched the entire camp for Alice, but could not find her. After determining Paul was not in his tent either, the

Indians immediately realized Paul must have helped her escape. Using non-verbal communication, the Indians made hand signals to one another pointing to the trees leading to the river. About two dozen Shawnee warriors ran swiftly into the woods with their hatchets in hand, poised and ready for action.

On the riverbank, Paul lifted Alice, still wrapped in the blanket, into the canoe. He wedged Alice between his pelts and climbed into the jam-packed canoe, all the while checking the trees to see if the Shawnee were in pursuit. He began rowing in a frenzy to get downriver.

About five minutes later, the approximately two dozen Shawnee warriors ran out of the woods onto the riverbank, exactly where Paul and Alice had just been. They looked down the river hoping to spot them, but saw nothing in the dark of night. The warriors walked back to their camp ending their brief but swift pursuit, disappointed and embarrassed at their failure in capturing the escaped prisoner and her abettor.

Unaware of the Shawnee's abrupt termination to their chase, Paul raced down the Little Miami River, rowing frantically throughout the night. At daybreak, Paul slowed down his frenetic pace. He had no choice at this point. His arms were like pieces of rubber after rowing all night. He was spent, but he felt intense gratification at having succeeded in his daring rescue and escape. Alice had fallen asleep in the blanket in the canoe. When she awakened in the morning, she was panicked. She immediately began searching for her Bible, which she quickly located in her dress pocket. She was deeply relieved at finding it.

"Are we safe?" she asked Paul.

"Yes," Paul responded. "We're forty or fifty miles downriver from the Shawnee camp."

"Won't they follow us?" she asked.

"No, don't worry," Paul said soothingly.

"But they were gonna burn me at the stake," Alice shot back. "Don't they still wanna kill me?"

"I imagine they do, but not enough to track you for a hundred miles or more," Paul said in a very matter of fact way. "They were goin' to kill you anyway. But now you have no worth."

"What about you?" Alice asked inquisitively.

"They got their goods from me," Paul said. "They made a pretty good deal. Just means my tradin' days are over. If they ever saw us again, they wouldn't hesitate none to kill us both."

"I'm afraid," Alice said.

"Don't be," Paul said reassuringly. "We ain't never goin' back anywhere near there again."

"Where are we goin'?" Alice asked.

"Kaskaskia," Paul answered.

"Kaskaskia? What's Kaskaskia?" Alice asked, genuinely confused.

"It's not a what!" Paul said. "It's a French settlement on the Mississippi River in the Illinois Territory, the only place we'll be safe."

"How far is it?" she asked.

"It takes almost a fortnight along the rivers," Paul explained. "I've made the trip many times. Get some rest."

Alice was somewhat relieved with Paul's assurances. She closed her eyes and fell asleep.

That night, Paul pulled the canoe onto the shore of the Ohio River. He awakened Alice and helped her out of the canoe. He made a campfire and the two relaxed by the fire eating beef jerky. He boiled some water in a kettle and poured a cup of coffee for Alice and himself.

"It was lucky I left some supplies in the canoe," Paul said to Alice.

"Yes, 'twas," she said as she took a sip of coffee.

"I don't even know your name," Alice said.

"My name is Paul L'Archevêque," Paul said. "The Shawnee just called me Larsh for short. What's your name?"

"I am Mrs. Alice Kincaid," she answered.

"Pleased to make your acquaintance, ma'am," Paul said.

"Mr. Larsh, how'd you happen to become a fur trader with the Shawnee?" Alice asked.

"I came from Montreal in Canada about three years ago and settled in Kaskaskia," he explained. "Nobody in Kaskaskia was tradin' with the Shawnee so I loaded up with tradin' goods and headed to the Ohio Valley. I've been tradin' with the Shawnee ever since, at least until now."

Alice finished her coffee and prepared herself for bed. She gazed up at the stars thinking of the evil acts she and her family experienced at the hands of the Shawnee during the last week.

"They are savages," Alice said as she rolled over to go to sleep.

Paul threw the remainder of his coffee from his cup into the fire. Paul watched Alice as she slept. He was relieved that she could at least manage to get to sleep after all she had been through. Paul felt nothing but deep sympathy for her. He had never known any human being who had faced so much trauma and heartbreak in such a short period of time. Paul was totally drawn to Alice. He admired her strength and determination, but knew she was severely depressed at having lost her entire family. He lay down on the other side of the fire, but had trouble falling asleep. His mind was consumed solely by his desire to protect and care for this woman.

The next day on the Ohio River, Paul rowed the canoe while Alice sat comfortably reading her Bible. Paul watched Alice from the rear of the canoe as she was seated in the front facing him. She glanced up from her Bible at Paul only for a second, revealing the slightest of smiles before resuming her reading. He continued rowing the canoe down the river for the remainder of the day while she read her Bible. Not a single word was spoken between them.

After covering about forty miles, Paul and Alice camped on the riverbank in the evening. As they ate fish by the campfire, Paul noticed Alice staring off into space. She was obviously overwhelmed by the recent events in her life. Paul was at first hesitant to ask her any questions regarding her ordeal, but his curiosity got the best of him.

Paul cautiously inquired, "What happened to Mr. Kincaid, if I may ask?"

Alice paused for a moment, as she was not sure she was ready to detail the terrifying hardships she underwent only days ago.

"The Indians raided our farmhouse in Jackson River, Virginia," Alice finally responded. "My husband, George, and me, was gettin' ready to put the children to bed. He was killed right away."

Alice did not cry as she began recounting the story. However, she abruptly stopped, seemingly unable to continue.

"I'm sorry," Paul said, perceiving how difficult it was for her to talk about it.

The blank expression on Alice's face remained as she stared straight ahead. She could not understand why her world had been turned upside down. She resumed her story, however, with specifics of her son's death.

"Then they killed my boy, David, 'cuz he wouldn't stop cryin'," she said. "'Twas as if they were givin' him a spanking, but instead they killed him. They brutally killed a small, scared, innocent little boy, simply 'cuz he couldn't stop cryin'."

Alice finally broke down and began to cry herself. Paul put his arm around her, awkwardly patting her head in an effort to soothe her.

She continued crying and said, "They killed my baby girl, Mary. And I'll never see my William again." Alice put her head deeper into Paul's sympathetic embrace.

"This pain is too unbearable," she said.

Paul did his best to try to ease her sadness. She continued sobbing as he laid her down on her blanket where she fell asleep. He went to the other side of the fire and lit his pipe. He gazed at Alice intently. He was falling in love with her, but knew she was too grief-stricken for him to make his feelings known. For now, he was just happy he could console her.

On the river the next day, Paul diligently continued rowing while Alice kept busy by reading her Bible. She appeared to be particularly contented with this activity. The bruises and cuts on her face were now beginning to heal. She and Paul had spoken briefly at times during their journey on the river, but by and large they had not had a great deal of conversation. Paul felt uneasy trying to talk with Alice, but he tried despite his insecurities.

"You love readin' that Bible, don't you?" he said.

"It gives me great comfort," she replied.

"Was it Mr. Kincaid's?" Paul asked.

"No, 'twas my mother's," she told him.

"Oh," Paul said.

Alice placed her Bible in her lap to speak to Paul, realizing she could not continue reading with his interruptions. She raised her eyebrows and pursed her lips, expressing to Paul without words that he now had her full attention.

Taking his cue, Paul asked, "I was just curious how you met Mr. Kincaid."

"George came to America from Scotland over ten years ago," she explained. "His ship sailed into New York. I lived there with my parents.

George had plans to settle in Virginia. I was
sixteen and George was twenty-six when we met.
We fell madly in love."

Paul nodded as he listened.

"I married him soon after he arrived in New
York and we left immediately for Virginia," she
continued. "My mother gave me her Bible when I
left. She said her mother had given it to her
when she had gotten married."

Alice paused again as she fondly reminisced
about happier times. Paul waited patiently for
her to resume the details of her life story. He
was enraptured with Alice's every word.

"George and me was very happy," she said.
"He was a good, honest, God-fearing man. I
loved him so."

Suddenly, Alice's mood changed. She became
despondent and melancholy. She leaned back and
closed her eyes, recalling her once joyful life
with George and how it had all disappeared in an
instant. Paul looked at her compassionately,
but had no idea what to say, so he said nothing.
He kept rowing down the river. She returned to
her reading.

After a long uncomfortable silence, Paul
said, "Read something aloud."

Alice obliged his request despite feeling slightly bothered. She flipped through the pages of her family Bible searching for an appropriate selection. After finding it, she realized she was about to recite a profound passage relating to the recent events and upheaval in her life.

"From Ecclesiastes, chapter three, verses one through four," Alice said. "For every thing there is a season, and a time for every purpose under the heaven: A time to be born, and a time to die; A time to plant, and a time to pluck up that which is planted; A time to kill, and a time to heal; a time to break down, and a time to build up; A time to weep, and a time to laugh; a time to mourn, and a time to dance."

After reading the passage, Alice looked steadily at Paul for his reaction. He thought about the meaning of the words, looking deep into her eyes for a brief moment to convey to her that he understood. Alice returned to reading silently. They said virtually nothing the rest of the day. Their only conversation consisted of Paul informing Alice they would be camping for the night.

The next day of their trip brought them to the only dangerous section on the Ohio River, the Ohio Falls. As the canoe approached the rapids leading to the falls, Paul warned Alice to hold on and to put her Bible in a safe place. Alice became alarmed.

"Are we in trouble?" she asked.

"Don't worry," Paul said. "It'll get a little rough for the next couple miles, but we'll be fine."

"It seems more than a bit rough," she said.

"The bumpy part will be at the falls," Paul said nonchalantly.

"What?" Alice said, now very concerned.

"It's only about a four-foot drop, as long as I can keep us in the middle of the river," Paul said. "Just hold onto your Bible."

"I hope you know what you're doing," she said.

"I've gone over these falls many times and I haven't sunk the canoe yet," Paul said confidently.

"Oh, my Lord," Alice responded.

"It should be a little drop and a slight jolt," Paul said. "As long as you hold on and brace yourself, you should be fine."

As they got closer to the falls, Paul

shouted to Alice, "Here it comes."

Alice made sure her Bible was secure in her pocket and she grabbed each side of the canoe in a tight grip with her hands. She closed her eyes as the canoe tipped down over the four-foot drop and crashed into the water below at a very high speed. Alice bounced a bit as they landed, but otherwise no harm was done to her, Paul, or the canoe. Paul navigated the canoe downriver as if nothing had happened.

"I told you it wouldn't be a problem!" Paul said smugly.

Days later, Paul and Alice finally arrived at the dock on the Mississippi River at Kaskaskia. Paul helped Alice out of the canoe and onto the dock. They headed toward town. Alice was still moving rather slowly, due partly to the abuse she endured, but also because she was just mentally worn to a frazzle. Her bruises and abrasions were nearly healed, but the remnants of her brutal thrashing remained upon her face. As Paul and Alice moved gingerly up the street in Kaskaskia, Guillaume spotted them from inside his store. Guillaume called to his wife, Ellen, to come outside with him. Upon seeing Alice, Ellen instinctively ran to her, grabbing her by the arm to assist her.

"This is Alice Kincaid," Paul said.

"Alice, these are my friends, Guillaume and Ellen Hennet.  They own the General Store."

"How do you do?" Alice said.

"We're fine, but you look like you've had a long journey," Ellen said.  "Let me help you, dear."

Ellen, already holding Alice with one arm, placed her other arm around Alice's waist to steady her and led her inside the General Store. The Hennets' home was adjacent to and a part of the same building as the store.

"Thank you, kindly," Alice said.

"What happened?" Guillaume asked Paul.

"The Shawnee killed Alice's husband and two of her children," Paul replied.  "They took Alice prisoner and were goin' to burn her at the stake the day after I arrived.  I snuck her out of camp and back to here.  I watched as they ran Alice through the gauntlet.  I thought they killed her.  Knocked her baby girl right out of her arms, killin' the poor little thing.  Her oldest son is still there, but the Shawnee have adopted him.  I couldn't get him out too.  I fear he will never be freed."

Paul suffered tremendous guilt in leaving William behind, but he knew deep down in his heart he had been powerless to save him. Paul recognized his good luck in rescuing Alice from the Indian camp. Had the Shawnee caught him, he would have been burning at the stake right alongside Alice.

Guillaume was wholly confounded at the dreadful story Paul had just described. "I've never heard of such a thing in my entire life," Guillaume said.

"I only know that my tradin' days are over," Paul sighed. "I cannot return to the Shawnee. They would kill me in a second if they ever saw me again. I broke their trust."

"You can work at the store if you like," Guillaume offered. "The settlement's been growing and I could use the help. Alice can stay here with us. Ellen would enjoy the female company and some help with the baby, too."

"Thank you, Guillaume," Paul said. "You're a right good friend to me."

"It's the least I can do for you after all you've been through. I've never heard of such a thing," Guillaume repeated, still flabbergasted by the experience his friend related.

# Chapter 5

Paul spent the next two and a half years in Kaskaskia waiting for Alice to move on from her shattered life. By the spring of 1759, he was still working for Guillaume in the General Store stocking shelves and helping customers. It was far less exciting than his trading days with the Shawnee Indians, but the tedium was tolerable due to his close proximity to Alice, who had been living with the Hennets during this time. Paul's wages from working in the store were only a pittance compared to the income he earned as a fur trader, but his priority now was to capture Alice's heart, not to increase his already sizable savings.

Paul had approached her on three separate occasions on the subject of matrimony. Alice had politely but firmly turned him down each time. Unfortunately for Paul, Alice did not seem the least bit enthusiastic concerning his plans for marriage, but this did not deter Paul.

Alice had been happily living with Guillaume and Ellen, often playing with their baby, Antoinette. Alice made her dolls and spent hours at a time with her, all the while imagining Antoinette was her own baby girl. However, Alice could not make the sorrow of losing her own family disappear completely. Mercifully, Alice had her own room in the

Hennets' house where she could retreat in her darkest moments, providing her the privacy to cry without anyone hearing her. As the years passed by, Alice seemed to be having fewer dark moments, engaging in more playing and less crying. Her grief would never entirely disappear, but it was beginning to subside.

One day during the spring of 1759, Paul was working in the back of the store stocking shelves with small flour barrels. Guillaume was taking care of a customer in the front of the store at the counter. The Hennets' living quarters could be accessed through their kitchen from the store. Ellen and Alice were in the kitchen seated at the table washing strawberries they had just picked. Ellen's baby, Antoinette, now a toddler, was walking around the table, her little face covered in juice from the strawberries she had eaten. After having finished stocking the shelves, Paul walked toward the front of the store past the open door to the kitchen, smiling at Alice, Ellen, and the toddler as he passed by.

Paul approached Guillaume who was behind the counter. Guillaume's grin stretched across his face as he realized Paul was on another quest to romance Alice. It was always the same, Paul's awkward stance, his slicked down hair, the twitchy way he rubbed his hands together, and the stupid, confused look upon his face gave him away every time. Guillaume could barely contain his laughter as he finished his sale with a customer before turning his attention to Paul. After the customer departed, Paul blurted out his all too familiar question to Guillaume.

"Has, has, has Alice said anything to you about me?" Paul nervously asked Guillaume.

"What on earth are you talking about?" Guillaume responded disingenuously, still grinning because he knew precisely where Paul was going with this conversation.

"You know exactly what I'm talking about," Paul said. "You know I've been in love with Alice since the day I took her away from the Shawnee."

"Oh, so you want to know if she'll marry you," Guillaume said facetiously. "I thought you told me you asked her ten times already and she said no."

"No, I asked her three times in the last two and a half years, the first time a few months after we got here, again six months later, and then about a year or so after that," Paul responded.

"Well, so she said no three times already," Guillaume said playfully, knowing full well

Alice had rejected Paul's request for matrimony exactly three times.

"Yeah, but each time she said she had strong feelings for me, but was still grievin' over her family," Paul said. "I don't know if I can take another rejection."

"It can't hurt to ask her," Guillaume said, holding back his laughter. "The worst she can say is no again. Shouldn't be a problem for you. You seem to have plenty of practice with rejection."

"That sure is the truth," Paul said, not even picking up on Guillaume's sarcasm. Paul was dead serious in his mission to marry Alice. He hardly even noticed that Guillaume was poking fun at him.

That night, Ellen and Alice cleaned up the kitchen after dinner. Guillaume stepped outside to get some more wood for the fireplace. After Guillaume came back in, Ellen picked up Antoinette from her highchair. The Hennet family withdrew to their bedroom while Alice retired to her bedroom in another corner of the house, all bidding each other goodnight. Alice sighed as she entered her room. She was longing for the same happiness the Hennet family enjoyed. As she lay there in bed, she recalled the cheerful times she had with her husband and their three beautiful children back on the farm in Virginia.

Meanwhile, Paul had just finished dinner and departed the restaurant up the street. He sauntered past the General Store on his way home. His mind was consumed with proposing marriage to Alice once again. He entered his lonely domicile and flopped down on his bed. He felt sad and frustrated at being alone. He stared at the ceiling as he lay in bed, his arm pressed across his forehead, thinking about his love for Alice. After a moment, he banged his fist into his palm, and with a new determination and confidence, jumped out of bed and out the door. He walked briskly up the street toward the General Store and behind it to a window at the Hennets' residence. Paul tapped on the window and awakened Alice.

"Paul, what are you doing here this time of night?" Alice asked, startled by his sudden presence at her bedroom window.

"Alice, I need to know if you're ever goin' to marry me," Paul told her. "You know I love you with all my heart. I would do anything for you. I understand you've been grievin' and I respect that. But you can't torture a man like this forever."

"I'll marry you, Paul," Alice said smiling

ear to ear. "I'm ready. I was just waitin' for you to ask me again."

Paul grabbed her by the shoulders and gave her a long passionate kiss through the window. She beamed at him following their kiss, then laughed lovingly at his elation.

"You drive me crazy, Alice Kincaid," Paul said to Alice in the tenderest way. "I love you so much. You've made me the happiest man on all o' God's green earth. I promise you'll never regret it!"

Paul leapt into the air in jubilation as he left her window and headed home.

Alice was smiling broadly herself, barely able to contain her joy. Paul's timing was perfect. Alice was finally ready to start her life over again and forget the terrible tragedies that had befallen her in the past. In the other room, Ellen was hard at work with her hand held firmly over Guillaume's mouth, as he was barely able to contain his laughter after listening to every word Paul had said from their open bedroom window. Once again, his friend put him into hysterics with his bumbling and unorthodox methods of courtship. However, this time Paul prevailed and Guillaume could not have been happier for him.

Two months later, Paul and Alice stood before the priest at the altar in the St. Anne's Catholic Church in Kaskaskia getting married. Paul was dressed in a black suit. Alice borrowed Ellen's loveliest blue gingham dress. It fit Alice beautifully, as she and Ellen were similarly built. Guillaume was the best man and Ellen was the matron of honor, both standing on the altar beside Paul and Alice.

Just before the ceremony started, little Antoinette, the flower girl at the wedding, handed Alice a bouquet of wildflowers that she and Ellen had picked. They were a little worn from being gripped tightly in the fist of a three-year-old, but well received by Alice who greatly appreciated the loving gesture. Alice became a little teary-eyed as she imagined her own lost baby girl.

For a brief moment, the melancholy thoughts of her dead husband and children almost overtook her. Yet she felt sure that George Kincaid would have wanted happiness for her again. She regained her composure quickly, realizing her dearly departed husband, George, would have supported her decision to remarry.

The priest asked, "Do you, Paul L'Archevêque, son of Paul Phillipe L'Archevêque, Master Cobbler, and of Angelique LeBoeuf, lawful spouses residing in Montreal, of the one part, take Alice Ann Dean Kincaid, daughter of William Dean and Sarah Campbell, lawful spouses residing in New York, of the other part, to be your lawfully wedded wife in the eyes of God?"

"I do," Paul said.

The priest continued, "Do you, Alice Ann Dean Kincaid, take Paul L'Archevêque to be your lawfully wedded husband in the eyes of God?"

"I do," Alice said.

The priest, concluding the nuptials, said, "With the power vested in me by the King's Almoner at Fort Quebec, and as the Pastorate of St. Anne's Catholic Church of Kaskaskia of the Illinois Territory in the year of our Lord, 1759, this nineteenth of June, I give Paul and Alice the nuptial blessing of our Mother Holy Church in the presence of Guillaume and Ellen Hennet, and all those gathered here, and I pronounce you in the name of God, the Almighty, man and wife. You may kiss the bride."

Paul kissed Alice sweetly on the lips. Guillaume and Ellen embraced the bride and groom. Antoinette danced around the couples waving a flower she'd picked up off the floor. The small number of people in the congregation moved forward to offer the bride and groom their congratulations. Alice and Paul held hands and

moved toward the exit of the church with their
delighted guests gathered around them.

# Chapter 6

In the spring of 1760, Paul and Alice were blessed with a baby boy they named Charles. The three of them resided in the same one-room house Paul had lived in since he first arrived in Kaskaskia back in 1753. Paul continued working at Guillaume's store, while Alice took care of little Charles at home. The L'Archevêque family was quite content in the peaceful and private confines of Kaskaskia.

Their comfortable life changed unexpectedly one cool afternoon in the autumn of 1760. Alice was at home as Charles lay asleep in his crib. She was relaxing by the fireplace in her rocking chair reading the Bible her mother had given her. A strong warm fire was burning in the hearth to chase away the chilly fall air. A knock came from the front door from the priest that married her. Alice invited him in. He was very serious in his manner. In contrast, Alice's demeanor was very cheerful.

"Good day, Father," she said.

"Good afternoon, Mrs. L'Archevêque," the priest said curtly as he glanced into the crib. "I trust you and your baby, Charles, are well."

"Yes, Father," Alice said. "We are both doing well."

The priest said, "You know, Mrs. L'Archevêque, your baby should be baptized in the Church as soon as possible. He is already over six months old."

Alice stopped reading and gaped at the priest, not believing what she was hearing.

"Father, I'm not Catholic," she said resentfully. "I was raised Presbyterian. My first husband, Mr. Kincaid, was also Presbyterian and our three children was all baptized in the Presbyterian Church back in Virginia."

"Stop woman," the priest shouted angrily. "You speak blasphemy."

"I am not speakin' blasphemy," Alice said, clearly taken aback by the priest's reaction. She placed her Bible in her lap, leaning back in her chair in complete astonishment.

The priest got a glimpse of the Bible.

"A King James Bible?" he said, his eyes bugging out. "You dare to read the King James Bible?"

"'Tis the Bible, Father," Alice responded rather indignantly. "Surely you don't object to my readin' the Bible?"

"You dare to read a Protestant Bible!" he said, now beside himself with feverish anger. The priest violently grabbed the Bible from Alice's lap and hurled it into the blazing fireplace.

"You madman," Alice screamed. Alice was in total disbelief at the priest's behavior. She could scarcely believe that a man of the cloth would desecrate a Holy Bible in such a way.

The priest stormed out of the house after his maniacal spectacle.

Alice was in shock for a moment before realizing it was her treasured Bible burning in the fireplace. She frantically tried to retrieve it by hand, but was unable to do so. She grabbed a poker and desperately struggled to save the Bible from the flames. By the time she was able to extricate it, however, her family heirloom had been charred beyond recognition. She retreated to her rocking chair, leaning over with her face buried in her hands, sobbing uncontrollably. Her baby, Charles, frightened by his mother's sobs, began to cry too. Alice rose from her chair and picked up the baby from the crib. She clutched her son as they both cried together in their small one-room house.

Later in the evening hours, Paul returned from working at the store. As he entered through the front door, Alice was seated in the rocking chair, her bloodshot eyes still filled with tears, rocking a now sleeping Charles.

"What's wrong?" Paul asked as he rushed to her side.

"The priest was here today," Alice replied calmly. "He took my Bible and threw it into the fire," as she pointed to her once beloved Bible by the fireplace, now unrecognizable.

"What?" Paul said incredulously. "Why would he do such a thing?"

"I told him my children wasn't baptized Catholic," Alice said tersely. "And because I was readin' a Protestant Bible, he just went crazy and threw it into the fire, destroyin' it... my mother's Bible!"

Alice put her head into Charles' soft neck, whose head was on her shoulder, and began crying again.

Paul became absolutely enraged. He rushed out the front door and ran up the street toward the St. Anne's Catholic Church.

The house beside the church belonged to the priest. Paul barged through the front door without knocking. The smug little priest was inside the house about ten feet away from a rather sizeable burning fire in the fireplace. The house was much larger than Paul's house. The priest was startled, but became increasingly frightened when he recognized it was Paul.  In his rage, Paul grabbed the priest firmly by his arm and collar, dragging him across the room toward the fireplace.

"No, no, please don't hurt me," the priest pleaded.

"I will do to you, sir, what you have done to my wife's Bible," Paul said vengefully.

Paul heaved the bullying priest forcibly into the fireplace.  The priest fell directly into the flames, shrieking in pain as he landed. Paul turned to leave through the front door, still angry and fuming, his adrenaline pumping. As he walked down the street back to his house, he began to calm down.  After realizing the gravity of what he had just done, he paused for a moment in front of his house before going in. It had dawned on him that there would be repercussions for his actions against the priest.  He would surely be facing harsh punishment for such an act.  A physical assault on a Catholic priest in a French settlement would not be tolerated for any reason.

As he entered his house, Alice was standing next to the crib rocking the baby tensely, deathly afraid of what might have transpired.

"What happened?" she asked apprehensively.

"Never mind," Paul said. "We have to get outta here. Get the baby and some food."

"What do you mean?" Alice asked. "What's happened?"

"We're leavin', now," Paul said.

"Leavin' where?" Alice again inquired.

"We're leavin' here," he said. "We're leavin' Kaskaskia for good. We don't have much time."

Paul moved the dresser and pulled up the floorboard. Paul dug into the dirt under the floorboard, pulled his box out, and removed all of his gold and silver coins.

Alice had the baby in her arms in a blanket, trying her best to gather clothes to take with her.

"Forget all that," Paul said to Alice. "Just bring the essentials for Charles. We're leavin' now."

Paul grabbed the mattress off the bed from the other side of the room. He hurriedly led Alice and the baby out the front door. As they rushed toward the dock to leave town, Paul looked back to see the priest crawling in the street on his hands and knees at the other end of town. Several townspeople were assisting him by this time. The priest's face and clothes were blackened from being thrown into the fire. Fortunately for Paul, the priest was so distressed and out of breath, he was not able to speak yet to identify Paul as his attacker.

Consequently, Paul and Alice had ample time to escape, but they still ran as quickly as they could to the dock where a raft was tied. Paul threw the mattress on the raft, helped Alice and the baby on board, and untied the rope. He began pushing the raft with an oar down the Mississippi River away from the Kaskaskia settlement on that dark, cloudy night. Luckily, no one in town seemed to notice their hasty departure.

By sunrise, Paul and his family were a safe distance away, more than forty miles from Kaskaskia heading south on the Mississippi River.

"Paul, did you kill that priest?" Alice asked.

"No, I didn't kill him," Paul replied, laughing to himself. "I just gave him a taste of his own medicine. I threw 'him' into the fireplace. He'll think twice before he ever tries to burn another Protestant Bible."

"I believe he will," Alice said, quite pleased that Paul defended her with such a vengeance.

"Where will we go?" she suddenly asked worriedly. "We're homeless!"

"I've been thinkin' about that," Paul said. "We can never go back to Kaskaskia or any other French settlement, or even to Canada. I'll be a wanted man by the French for assaulting that priest."

"We can't live out here in the wilderness," Alice said.

"I know," Paul agreed. "We have to go back east to live."

"You can't live among the English," Alice said. "They're at war with the French."

"Not for long," Paul said.

"What do you mean?" Alice asked.

"I mean the French have all but lost the war," Paul said. "The news in Kaskaskia was that the English armies had retaken all the forts in the east, Fort Niagara, Fort Quebec...Fort Duquesne is now Fort Pitt. They beat the French in Montreal, took control of Canada, and it'll only be a matter time before the war is officially over. The fightin' is over."

"Yes, but how is a Frenchman named L'Archevêque goin' to live among the English?" Alice asked.

"That's easy," Paul replied. "I'll lose my accent and change my name. The Shawnee called me Larsh. I liked that. Far easier to say than L'Archevêque anyway."

"So where exactly will we go?" Alice asked.

"The Ohio River runs all the way to Pennsylvania," Paul explained. "I've enough money saved to buy us a farm."

"But you've never farmed before," Alice said.

"Yeah, and I'd never done no fur tradin' before neither," Paul said smirking, confident of his abilities to succeed in any endeavor.

# Chapter 7

A couple days later, Paul was steering the raft east on the Ohio River. Paul was paddling against a slight current, maybe a half a mile an hour at the most. Nevertheless, it was slightly more strenuous for Paul navigating a raft with three people against the current than rowing his canoe by himself. He had made this trip numerous times along the same exact route on his way to trade with the Shawnee Indians. This time, however, he would not be veering north on the Little Miami River to Chief Black Hoof's camp. He would stay on the Ohio River on the route back to Pennsylvania where he had passed through seven years before on his way to Kaskaskia. Paul would be starting a new life once again, except this time with Alice and Charles.

In the early portion of their long journey, they had to navigate the Ohio Falls. Alice was lying on the blanket cuddling the baby. She had tied Charles to her chest with some strips of fabric she had ripped from her apron. Alice was afraid the active little baby would slip off the edge of the raft and drown in the water before his father could save him. As they approached the falls, Paul steered the raft to the shore.

"We have to go on foot along the riverbank," Paul said as the raft bumped onto the shoreline.

Alice cautiously tiptoed off the raft onto the riverbank clutching Charles.

"You'll have to drag the mattress," Paul said to Alice. "I'll drag the raft. It's about two miles to get back to calm waters."

Alice dutifully followed Paul along the shore as he dragged the heavy raft. She had one hand on Charles, who was still tied to her apron, as she pulled the mattress. Paul had propped up the raft on his back and shoulders, grabbing a hold of the top of it with his hands, hunching over a bit to support the weight of it, while he dragged it behind him. After two miles of this strenuous effort, Paul and Alice were dog-tired. Charles, on the other hand, was full of energy, laughing and clapping his hands, totally unaware of his parents' weariness. Soon, Alice and Paul were laughing too, despite their fatigue.

Once they were past the rapids, Paul dropped the raft on the riverbank and prepared to make camp for the night. Alice was relieved to drop her heavy load too. She immediately laid Charles on the mattress and plopped down next to him in exhaustion.

That night, Paul and Alice sat by the

campfire.  A squirrel Paul caught cooked on a
stick over the fire.  The baby was asleep on the
mattress next to Alice.

"When will we get to the end of this
river?" Alice asked.

"Maybe a few weeks, I think," Paul
answered.  "We've been lucky.  As long as we
don't run across any Indians, I think we'll
survive.  It's always a little slower goin'
upstream, but there's no more falls or rapids.
The river is pretty calm the rest of the way."

"I've been thinkin' a lot of William,"
Alice said.  "I wonder if he's still alive."

"If he is, he's no longer the boy he once
was," Paul said.

"That's the pain of it all," Alice said.
"I keep imaginin' he's become like the animals
that killed his father and baby brother and
sister."

"Don't think of it," Paul responded.  "If
he is alive and has become a Shawnee, there
ain't nothin' nobody can do now."

"I fear for our little Charles," Alice
said, stroking the baby's head.

"Nothin' will ever happen to Charles, not

as long as I am still alive," Paul said.

"I believe you, Paul," Alice said, encouraged by his remarks. "I feel safe with you. I love you so much."

"I love you too, Alice," he said.

Paul took his knife out, pulled the stick with the squirrel on it away from the fire, and cut pieces of meat from its carcass. He handed a piece to Alice. She began eating it with her hands. He cut a piece for himself and ate it off his knife. Getting something to eat every day was becoming critical, as they were both famished having come so far on their journey with still weeks to go. Paul and Alice both knew the remainder of the trip would be long and difficult. They were eager to reach Pennsylvania and to bring their voyage to a close.

After traveling for weeks on the river, they arrived at a fork in the Ohio River at Fort Pitt in Pennsylvania. The Ohio River intersected with the Allegheny River to the north and the Monongahela River to the south. The newly built Fort Pitt was located at the intersection of the river behind old Fort Duquesne, now demolished. Fort Duquesne had been situated closer to the river, but only a shell of the old French fort remained in front of Fort Pitt. Paul steered the raft into the Allegheny River, then into a canal, docking near the entrance to Fort Pitt. Paul and his family disembarked where a British soldier stopped them asking them their business. When Paul indicated they were there to purchase supplies, they were allowed to proceed into the fort.

Paul and his family travelled almost one thousand miles from Kaskaskia to Fort Pitt. Miraculously, they had avoided any danger or mishaps on the river, and more importantly, they had not encountered any hostile Indians. Although Indians at various places occupied both banks of the Ohio River, they made it safely to Fort Pitt without confronting any Indians or any serious obstacles.

Fort Pitt bustled with activity from both British soldiers and civilians. Paul quickly located the general store to purchase much needed supplies. Alice, looking so disreputable, was ashamed of her appearance. However, she was so relieved to be off the raft that she quickly overcame her embarrassment. Paul and Alice were wearing dirty ragged clothes after weeks on the river. Paul had grown a full beard and his hair was long and shaggy. Neither of them noticed how badly the other smelled anymore. Unfortunately, the stench was quite evident to everyone else.

The owner of the store gave them a long look, taking note of their unflattering and disheveled appearance.

"What can I do for you stranger?" the owner asked.

"I need some supplies, some shoes and clothes for my wife, and some blankets to begin with," Paul answered.

The owner gathered some blankets and put them on the counter. He pointed to the other side of the store and said, "You'll find some ladies' clothin' over there."

Alice walked in that direction with the baby, picking up some clothing with her one free arm to inspect them. Paul found some tin plates, eating utensils, a kettle, and a small flour barrel, which he placed on the counter.

"Do you sell Bibles?" Paul asked.

"Yeah, we have them over there," the owner said, pointing across the store to a stack of Bibles.

Alice looked over at Paul, extremely pleased at his thoughtfulness. She and Paul smiled at one another from across the store. Paul retrieved one of the Bibles from the stack. As he inspected the brand new book, he noticed

"King James Bible" clearly printed on the binding.

"Alice, look," Paul hollered as he held up the Bible pointing to the printing.

"I see," Alice said smiling broadly from across the store. "Thank you, Paul. You're a dear."

Paul returned to the owner on the other side of the store and placed the new Bible and the rest of his purchases on the counter.

"Where might I find some good farm land in these parts?" Paul asked the owner.

"Fayette County, down the Monongahela River about forty miles," the owner responded. "The farmers down there occasionally supply me with some whiskey. A lot of maize and apples gits growed down there."

Alice brought some clothes and shoes up to the counter, including a new apron to replace the one she ripped up to tie Charles to her on the raft. She placed them on Paul's pile of items being purchased. The owner counted up the cost of what was there. He was a bit skeptical as to whether Paul had the money to pay since Paul's appearance did not reflect any level of prosperity on his part.

"Twenty pounds, mister," the owner said with suspicion.

Paul reached into his pocket and placed eight French gold coins and eight French silver coins on the counter. The owner looked surprised, but pleased. He recognized the French coins as having the same value as twenty pounds in British sterling. After all, money was money. He happily picked up the coins and placed it in his cash box under the counter. Paul gathered up his purchases as he and Alice headed for the door to leave.

The owner asked, "What's your name?"

"Larsh, Paul Larsh," he said.

Paul glanced over to Alice, giving her a wry smile at having used his shortened name for the very first time.

"Well, Mr. Larsh, I do know a farmer with four hundred acres down in Fayette County who wants to sell and head back to Philadelphia where he come from," the owner said. "You could probably git it for a right fair price. His name's Jacob Rummel. His farm is about ten miles southwest of Springhill Township in Fayette County, a few miles from the Monongahela River near George's Creek."

"Thanks for the tip, mister," Paul said.

After carefully placing their new purchases onto their raft, they continued their journey down the Monongahela River south from Fort Pitt. As Paul and Alice came closer to their final destination, they looked into the distance to the east from the river. Farmhouses were dotted throughout the hilly countryside. The town of Springhill could be seen in the distance. Paul would later purchase the three hundred and seventy acre farm called "Apple Orchard" from Jacob Rummel. Rummel's asking price for Apple Orchard was three hundred pounds British sterling, but he accepted Paul's three thousand livres in French gold and silver. The payment for the farm was just about everything Paul had left from his savings as a fur trader and as a clerk at the General Store in Kaskaskia over the last seven years.

Paul and Alice were excited to begin their new life at Apple Orchard, but they could not help feeling guilt and remorse for abruptly leaving their good friends, the Hennets, back in Kaskaskia. Obviously, circumstances prevented them from saying goodbye, but the fact that they would most likely never see Guillaume, Ellen, and Antoinette again, who had become like family, would haunt them for the rest of their lives.

After the Treaty of Paris of 1763 was

signed officially ending the French and Indian War, the French lost all of its territories in mainland North America to the British. French civil officials immediately left Kaskaskia, creating anarchy in the settlement. Nearly all of its inhabitants, including the Hennets, abandoned the town as well.

# Chapter 8

At the Shawnee Indian camp on the Little Miami River, William Kincaid had reached the age of fourteen years. Dressed like a Shawnee warrior, he looked more like an Indian than a white man. In fact, by this time, no one could mistake William for being anything other than an Indian. He was riding barebacked on a horse with the other young Indian boys who were also on horseback. They rode out of the Shawnee camp and through a meadow near the woods, pulling arrows from their quivers and shooting at game. William shot an arrow hitting a deer in full stride right through its neck. William and the other Indian boys rode swiftly to the slain deer. William slid off his mount in mid-gallop to inspect his kill, demonstrating remarkable agility and horsemanship for someone his age.

William had developed exceptional skill riding and hunting while being raised by the Shawnee during the last five years. William approached the fallen deer with pride. The other Indian boys followed to see the deer William had so expertly killed.

"You are deadly with the bow, Blue Jacket," one of the Indian boys said to William. "No one can shoot like you."

William smiled with great satisfaction.

William was clearly the leader of the group. He directed the other Indian boys to secure the deer carcass on the back of a horse. Back at camp, Chief Black Hoof and the tribe were gathering for a raiding party, making all necessary preparations for battle. William and the other young Indians returned to camp with the slain deer. Chief Black Hoof waved to William, motioning for him to come to speak with him. William jumped off his horse and went directly to Chief Black Hoof.

"I see you have had good hunting today, Blue Jacket," Chief Black Hoof said.

"Yes Great Chief...I shot him through the neck at a full gallop," William said proudly as he pointed to the deer he killed.

"You are growing into a man now, Blue Jacket," the Chief said. "You are ready to join the war party. They will be leaving soon. Prepare yourself young warrior and fight bravely."

"I will not disappoint you," William said.

Later on, William mounted his horse with the war party as they readied to leave camp. With war paint adorning his face, William had prepared with the rest of the warriors for battle. Chief Black Hoof addressed the war party prior to their departure.

"Fight like great and fierce warriors to keep the white man away," Chief Black Hoof declared.

The war party rode out of camp making high-pitched shrieks and yelps as they galloped away, clearly fervent about their mission.  After nearly a day's ride east, they reached the Ohio River.  They camped and rested for a few hours before riding into southwestern Pennsylvania at dusk.

Subsequently, they approached a white settlement and spotted an isolated farmhouse. The war party advanced on horseback toward the residence, hollering and shrieking in their attack.  The Indians shot their arrows, some lit with fire, at the lonesome-looking dwelling. William was exhilarated to be a participant, shooting his arrows as accurately as he could. The burning arrows landed on the outside walls and on the thatched roof, spreading flames quickly.  The terrified residents of the house fired their guns from within the now burning walls of their home.  The farmers managed to shoot two of the Shawnee warriors off their horses, killing them both.  William was not deterred by the deaths of his Indian brothers, nor was he fearful of the defenders from within the house.  William knew he must not disappoint

Chief Black Hoof.

The occupants of the house were initially successful in holding off the Indians until the structure finally became fully engulfed in flames. The father and his adult son ran out of their fiery home shooting their musket rifles. They each got off a shot, but missed in their haste. William, taking dead aim, shot the father through the heart with an arrow. The son pulled out his knife from his waist band to continue the fight, but the other Shawnee warriors immediately shot him with two more arrows, one through the throat and the other through the heart. He fell to the ground dead before he could inflict any more harm to his attackers.

A fair-haired mother and her young daughter ran from the house behind the two men. Immediately after killing the father and son, two Shawnee warriors seized the women, simultaneously scalping them for their prized blonde locks. The mother and the girl screamed in agony and fell to the ground, blood streaming from their heads. The house continued burning. No one else came out.

William jumped off his horse to take his first scalp. He was disappointed to find the father he had just killed was bald. The other Shawnee warriors laughed at William. The Indian who killed the son laughed too as he scalped the wavy brown hair from the son's head. Unsure of what to do, William hovered over the bald father briefly before climbing back onto his horse. He was utterly discouraged at not having gotten his first scalp.

The two slain Shawnee warriors were flung on a horse to be taken away for later burial. As the Shawnee war party rode away from the carnage they inflicted on the family at the farmhouse, they raised their arms, howling and squealing, elated with their victory.

William felt absolutely no remorse after killing a man for the first time. In fact, he suffered no guilt or shame at all for his involvement in the brutal murder of an entire family. Instead, he felt the same pride as he had earlier in the day when killing a deer. William's only concern now was to be a Shawnee warrior worthy of Chief Black Hoof's approval and admiration. William viewed himself exclusively as a Shawnee Indian, not a white man. He firmly believed that the white settlers were infringing on Shawnee lands. His former identity, William Kincaid, was just a faint memory. He was, for all intents and purposes, a full-fledged Shawnee Indian warrior, forever more to be known as "Blue Jacket."

# Chapter 9

By 1772, Paul had been working the Apple Orchard farm for twelve years. On this particular day, he was chopping wood outside his farmhouse. He was now thirty-eight years old with more gray in his hair and looking more worn with age. Paul was dressed in store-bought farmer's clothes instead of the buckskin attire he wore years before when he was a fur trader. His son, Charles, now twelve years old, was feeding chickens by the barn. Alice came outside to get water from the well. Alice was now forty-two years old and appearing more middle-aged than the pretty woman of years earlier.

Paul said to his son, "Charles, when I'm finished chopping this wood, I'll need help in the barn."

"Sure, Pop," Charles said.

Paul stacked up some wood and headed for the barn. Charles followed him in. A large still was set up in the middle of the barn for making corn whiskey. The fire under the copper pot of the still was flickering out. Paul put some wood under it to get the fire going again.

The still for making whiskey was quite a simple contraption. Most of the farmers used the same method, known as distillation. First, fermented liquid was poured into a copper pot. In this case, corn was mashed into a liquid. The pot was capped and sealed, then heated. As the liquid inside the pot heated up, the alcohol in the liquid boiled first. Alcohol boiled at a lower temperature than water, and then turned to vapor. The alcohol vapor rose up into the head of the still and was drawn off into a tube and into a coil. The coil was submerged in cool water, condensing the alcohol vapors back into liquid. The liquid alcohol ran out of the coil and dripped into a glass collection jar.

"Hey, Pop, this jar is full," Charles said, as he picked up a full glass jar of whiskey and replaced it with an empty glass jar under the coil of the still.

"Put that whiskey in the barrel, Charles," Paul instructed. "Then mash up some more of the corn so we can fill up the pot."

"Yes, Pop," Charles said dutifully.

The copper pot had to be emptied and cleaned before the next batch could begin. The leftover corn mash from the copper pot was used to feed the livestock. Paul and Charles continued working methodically together, preparing the corn mash for the next collection of whiskey from the still. Every day, jars of whiskey were collected and emptied into barrels. After months of this work, Paul had more barrels of whiskey than he could sell.

Later on that evening, the Larsh family finished their meal at the dinner table in the farmhouse.

"That was very tasty," Paul said to Alice.

"I'm glad you enjoyed it," Alice said as she started clearing the table, stacking plates and grabbing spoons.

"Let me help you, Mother," Charles said, picking up the remaining utensils.

"Excuse me," Paul said, getting up from the table and lighting his pipe.

At that moment, the sound of horses galloping outside the house was heard.

"Who's that this late?" Alice asked anxiously. She suddenly had a flashback of the Indian raid in Jackson River on her family in 1756. She felt complete and utter panic, imagining the sound of the horses outside was another Indian raid on her home.

"It's nothin' to worry about, Alice, it's just our neighbors, Isaac and Jim," said Paul. "I asked Isaac yesterday when I saw him in town for him and Jim to stop by after dinner tonight to discuss some business."

"Thank God," Alice said.

"What's the matter, Alice?" Paul asked.

"Oh nothing, I just couldn't imagine who might be callin' this time of night," she said, not revealing to Paul the real sense of dread she had just experienced.

Isaac Griffin was Paul's best friend. Jim was his only son, a handsome, tall, sixteen-year-old. Isaac's farm was located just a few miles away. Isaac and Paul both produced whiskey from their crops, their primary source of income. Paul opened the door as Isaac and Jim were getting off their horses.

"Good evening, Isaac...Jim," Paul said.

"Paul, Alice, Charles, how are you this evening?" Isaac asked as he entered the house.

"I am well, thank you, Isaac," Alice said.

"I am well, sir," Charles also said.

Jim stood behind his father, taking his hat off as he entered. Jim acknowledged the Larshes with a nod.

"Ma'am," Jim said, greeting Alice.

"Can I get you men somethin'?" asked Alice. "We've just finished our meal, but I'll be glad to fix somethin' up for you and Jim."

"No thank you, Alice," Isaac said. "Mighty nice of you, but Mrs. Griffin already prepared us a delicious meal."

"How about some apple cider?" Alice asked.

"No thank you, Alice," Isaac said. "We're fine."

"How is Mary?" Alice asked.

"She's well," Isaac said. "She sends her best."

Isaac sat down next to Paul who was now sitting by the fireplace smoking his pipe. Isaac leaned into Paul to speak to him.

"I've got my whiskey ready to go, Paul," Isaac said. "You know I got twice as much as I can sell."

"Yeah, I've got the same problem," Paul replied. "That's what I wanted to talk to you about. We've been working this farm for twelve years and I've barely saved any money at all."

"We're doing all right," Alice chimed in as she continued cleaning up the kitchen.

"I'm not used to just doing all right," Paul said. "When I was tradin' with the Shawnee, I always had plenty of money. I put all my money in this farm. After twelve years of hard work, more years than I ever did fur tradin', I should have something to show for it besides a few dollars, a glut of whiskey, and too many apples I can neither sell nor eat."

Jim's eyes lit up at Paul's mention of Indians and fur traders.

"Tell us more about the Injuns, Mr. Larsh," Jim requested.

"That was a long time ago, Jim," Paul said with a laugh.

"I met some fur traders at Fort Pitt," Jim said. "They say the Shawnee are a proud people and just want to protect their right to live on the land of their ancestors."

"That's true, Jim," Paul replied.

"Jim's become fascinated with the redskins and the fur traders it seems," Isaac said, visibly annoyed. "He needs to concentrate more on workin' the farm."

Isaac looked up at Jim with a frown, clearly exasperated with Jim's admiration for the Indians. He turned back to speak with Paul, returning the conversation again to their whiskey production.

"Problem is Paul, we don't have enough folks to sell to," Isaac said in a somewhat frustrated fashion. "We can't get enough whiskey to Fort Pitt. Tryin' to take a wagon over those rocky hills and across a couple of rivers is damn near impossible."

Isaac immediately looked at Alice apologetically for his cursing.

"Pardon me, ma'am," Isaac said.

Alice just smiled, conveying her recognition of his acknowledgement of swearing.

"We need to send our whiskey up the river by boat," Paul said. "We could make a fortune shippin' whiskey up and down the river."

"Yeah, but where do we get the boats?" Isaac inquired.

"We build 'em," Paul answered.

"Build 'em?" Isaac asked skeptically.

"That's right," Paul said. "We build 'em. You and me! If I can build a canoe, I can surely make a flatboat."

"Well, my clever friend," Isaac said. "If

we build flatboats, how do we get the boats to the river from here?"

"We don't build 'em here," Paul replied. "We go to the river and build 'em there."

Isaac sat scratching his head considering Paul's suggestion.

"If you say so," Isaac said, still puzzled at how this could be accomplished.

"We could move every barrel of whiskey we had by flatboat," Paul explained. "We could go north to Fort Pitt and beyond, and south down the Monongahela River at the same time."

"Sounds like a good idea, Paul," Isaac said. "If you think we can do it, then I'm in."

Some days later, Paul, Charles, Isaac, and Jim began building a flatboat at the mouth of George's Creek on the Monongahela River. After working every day for two months, they had completed two flatboats and built a dock. They were now ready to unload their barrels of whiskey from wagons onto the new flatboats. Shortly thereafter, Isaac and Jim headed north on the Monongahela River in their flatboat loaded with whiskey barrels. Paul and Charles headed south in the other flatboat with their load of whiskey. Paul and Isaac had accomplished their goal and subsequently their business grew rapidly. They now supplied whiskey to Fort Pitt and other settlements along the Monongahela and Allegheny Rivers, bringing in more money than ever.

# Chapter 10

Some months later during the afternoon, Paul and Isaac were seated on the porch of Paul's farmhouse, relaxing and smoking their pipes.

"It's good to be prosperous again," Paul said to Isaac.

"Again?" Isaac said. "This is a first for me."

"We could build a couple more flatboats, I think," Paul said.

"Why?" Isaac asked. "We're movin' and sellin' all the whiskey we can make."

"We could move a lot more goods up and down the river with two more boats," Paul said.

"Yeah, but we don't make that much whiskey!" Isaac responded.

"No, I'm talkin' about other folks' goods," Paul said. "We could charge other people to ship their goods."

"Good idea," Isaac said.

Movement in the field distracted Paul. He noticed Jim and Charles some distance away from the house, waving goodbye.

"What are those two up to now?" Paul wondered.

"The boys are goin' huntin'," Isaac said.

"That's good," Paul said. "I'm glad Jim looks out for Charles. He's like a big brother to him. We've been so busy makin' and sellin' whiskey, I've been neglectin' Charles."

"Yeah, but you've been workin' together," Isaac noted.

"I just tell Charles what to do," Paul said. "I ain't spent no time with him other than business. That ain't no way to bond with your son."

A couple of hours later around sundown, Jim and Charles, each carrying a musket, looked for game as they walked through the woods near the Monongahela River.

"This is the life for me, hunting in the woods," Jim said to Charles. "I don't want to be no farmer making whiskey all my life. I want to do something excitin', like your father did when he was young."

"Pop don't talk too much about his days tradin' with the Injuns," Charles said. "My ma don't like him to. She hates the Injuns, 'specially the Shawnee. She says they ain't nothin' but killers."

"If they're killin', it's only 'cuz they's just protectin' what's rightfully theirs," Jim said. "They lead an excitin' life livin' off the land the way they do. And I don't mean like makin' corn whiskey and apple cider. Not that kind of livin' off the land. Just for a few measly dollars. They's got deeper meaning in what they do."

"I reckon," Charles said.

Jim and Charles wandered out of the woods toward George's Creek near the river. Charles spotted a beaver at the edge of the creek and fired his musket, but missed. Jim cocked his musket and slowly took aim. He hit the beaver square in the head.

"Wow, you got that critter good!" Charles exclaimed. "You're a crack shot, Jim."

"Yeah, I reckon I am," Jim said confidently.

At that moment, a small band of five Shawnee Indians rode out of the woods to the creek behind where Jim and Charles were standing. An Indian jumped off his horse and took their guns. Jim was absolutely unafraid and seemed secretly thrilled he was finally face to face with the Indians whom he so admired.

Charles, on the other hand, was petrified, believing he was going to be killed. The Indian motioned with his hand for Jim and Charles to get on the backs of the horses.

"Get on the horses," the Indian said in his Shawnee language as he continued motioning.

Neither Jim nor Charles understood Shawnee, but they both understood his meaning. Jim appeared excited to go, while Charles was clearly not. They each climbed on the back of the horses. The Indians rode the horses across the creek before crossing the Monongahela River a short distance away and riding deep into the open wilderness.

At Paul's farmhouse later that evening, Paul, Alice, Isaac, and Mary were waiting anxiously for Jim and Charles to return home. They became more upset with every passing minute, especially Alice and Mary. They feared the worst.

"Those boys shoulda' come back hours ago," Isaac said. "You know the Shawnee have been seen on the other side of the river recently. We shoulda' warned those two boys. I hope they didn't wander off too far."

"If they're not back by mornin', we'll go out and find them," Paul added. "No sense in goin' out now in the dark.  We can track them at daybreak."

Alice was becoming hysterical, bawling uncontrollably as she sat in her rocking chair.

"You've got to find my Charles," Alice told Paul as she continued crying.  "I can't go through this again.  I can't lose another one of my boys.  I just can't."

"We'll find him," Paul said resolutely as he patted Alice on her back trying to calm her. "I promise."

At a small Shawnee Indian camp in the wilderness that same evening, Blue Jacket, now twenty-five years old, waited for the return of the band of five Indians.  A dozen other Shawnee Indians were in the camp already.  The five Indians rode into camp late in the evening with the boys.  One of the Indians jumped off his horse and approached Blue Jacket.

"We have prisoners," the Indian told Blue Jacket.

The other four Indians dismounted their horses with Jim and Charles.  Jim was totally unfazed and looked pleased to be standing in front of Blue Jacket.  Charles, on the other hand, was not hiding his fear.  He looked like a scared rabbit.

"We will take them back with us," Blue Jacket said, speaking in Shawnee to the band of Indians.

Jim did not understand a word Blue Jacket said, but he knew the Indians were not letting them go. Jim figured they must have ridden twenty miles west of the river and that their main camp was probably another day's ride to the west.

"I will gladly go, but my friend cannot," Jim proposed.

Blue Jacket was taken aback by Jim's forthright manner, but at the same time he was intrigued with what the brash boy had to say.

"Speak, young one," Blue Jacket said in English.

"His ma's already lost a son to the Shawnee," Jim told Blue Jacket.

Charles was surprised at hearing this astounding piece of information. His mother had never spoken a word to him of her past or her family from her first marriage.

"How do you know of such things?" Blue Jacket asked, still speaking in English.

"Charles' pa done told it to my pa, who's

his good friend," Jim answered. "My pa told me that Charles' ma's whole family was killed by the Shawnee, exceptin' for her oldest son who was taken prisoner and raised by the Shawnee. Charles is the only son she's got left. Charles' pa done rescued Charles' ma from the Shawnee back when he was fur tradin' with the Shawnee way before Charles was even born."

"By what name is Charles' mother called?" Blue Jacket inquired.

"Mrs. Larsh, Mrs. Alice Larsh," Jim said.

"What does Alice Larsh look like?" asked Blue Jacket.

Jim paused to think, trying to describe her appearance as accurately as possible, and said, "I reckon you'd say she's a handsome woman, dark haired, and middle-aged."

"How did she escape from the Shawnee?" Blue Jacket further probed.

"Well, like I done said, my pa told me Mr. Larsh was fur tradin' with the Shawnee and done seen her and her children runnin' the gauntlet. They was goin' to burn her at the stake 'til Mr. Larsh rescued her. He couldn't git her son out too."

Blue Jacket recognized that Jim was

describing Alice Kincaid, Blue Jacket's own mother, but he gave no indication of this revelation. Blue Jacket also knew that the small boy standing before him, Charles, was in fact his half-brother. Neither Jim nor Charles had any inkling that Blue Jacket was formerly William Kincaid.

Blue Jacket turned to the band of Indians in the camp, and said in Shawnee, "We will leave tomorrow."

Blue Jacket spoke to Jim directly in English, "You will come with us, but I will return your young friend, Charles, to his mother and home."

At daybreak at Paul's farmhouse, Paul and Isaac mounted their horses, armed with their muskets, and rode toward the wooded area near George's Creek and the Monongahela River. As they arrived in the same area where Jim and Charles were the day before, Paul located a trail of hoof prints from the horses and footprints from the Indians and the boys.

"They were here," Paul said. "Several horses, too. The Indians have taken them, most likely the Shawnee. They left toward the river."

"Should we get some help," Isaac asked.

"No, there's not time," Paul responded. "We'll never catch up to them if we don't get movin' now. It's goin' to be a tough enough task as it is. Let's go, and quickly."

"I'm just followin' you, my friend," Isaac said. "You know these Injuns better than I do."

Isaac wasn't letting on to Paul, but he was extremely worried and unnerved. Paul stayed calm, but resolved. The two headed across the river and rode into the wilderness.

At the same time, Blue Jacket was riding across the wilderness with Charles on the back of his horse, heading back to the Monongahela River. Paul and Isaac rode toward them from the other direction in the east. They saw one another and rode directly toward each other's location. Isaac retrieved his musket and pointed it at Blue Jacket when they finally came face to face.

"Don't, Isaac," Paul said as he motioned to Isaac to lower his musket.

Isaac did not lower his musket. He appeared to want to kill Blue Jacket at the first chance. Charles jumped off Blue Jacket's horse and ran to safety, climbing on to the back of his father's horse.

"I have come in peace," Blue Jacket said in

124

English. "I am Blue Jacket. I have brought the boy for you to take back to his mother."

Paul realized immediately that Blue Jacket was William Kincaid. Paul remembered William wearing a blue hunting jacket when he was taken prisoner by the Shawnee at the age of nine. Paul subsequently heard Chief Black Hoof christen him with the name.

"What in tarnation is goin' on?" Isaac asked Paul.

"William?" Paul asked Blue Jacket.

Blue Jacket did not respond. Paul glanced down to see several scalps attached to Blue Jacket's waistband.

Isaac was getting exceedingly upset.

"Where's my boy?" Isaac asked in a slow and deliberate manner with his musket pointed directly at Blue Jacket.

"If your son is the tall one, he is safe with the Shawnee," Blue Jacket calmly answered. "He is not returning."

"Damned if he ain't!" Isaac said, cocking his rifle ready to shoot. "I'll shoot you right between the eyes, you lily-livered varmint."

"Don't, Isaac," Paul pleaded. "They'll

kill Jim for sure if this one doesn't come back."

Isaac contemplated this suggestion for a moment before realizing Paul was absolutely right in his assumption.

"All right," Isaac said as he lowered his musket.

"He wants to stay with the Shawnee," Blue Jacket said assertively.

"I don't believe you, you redskin bastard," Isaac said.

"It's true, Mr. Griffin," Charles confirmed. "Jim wants to stay with the Injuns. He done said so."

"Damn you Injuns to hell," Isaac said as he uncocked his musket. Isaac lowered his head in obvious despair, almost wanting to cry.

"Do not follow," Blue Jacket ordered.

Blue Jacket turned his horse and rode west from where he had come.

"Let's go home," Paul said.

After arriving back at the farmhouse later that night, Charles ran to his mother's arms.

"My dear boy, don't ever scare me like that again," Alice said to Charles as she hugged him. "I could not stand to lose you too. Thank the good Lord you're back home."

"I've seen William," Paul told Alice.

"What?" she said dumbfounded.

"He's a Shawnee warrior named Blue Jacket," Paul explained. "He was wearin' a blue jacket when the Shawnee took him, remember?"

Alice nodded yes.

"He brought Charles back and said to return him to his mother," continued Paul.

"Where is he?" she asked. "If he's alive, we must get him so he can come home."

"Alice, William is a Shawnee warrior," Paul said firmly. "He ain't comin' back. He will never come back. He is one of them. He no longer belongs with whites."

"Oh, how can this be?" Alice said crying as she became distraught at this realization.

## Chapter 11

By 1787, a small town had grown up around Paul and Isaac's boat building business at the mouth of George's Creek on the Monongahela River. The town became known as Wilson Point. The small building by the dock on the river had a wooden sign on it that read, "Larsh-Griffin Shipping."

One day, Paul was working in his office with a customer who was arranging to have his goods shipped up river to Fort Pitt. Isaac was at another desk behind Paul doing paperwork. Charles, now twenty-seven years old, came in to the office. He waited for his father to finish with the customer. As Paul concluded his business, the customer departed out the front door.

"Pop, we need to talk," Charles said.

"Sure," Paul said.

"I'm goin' out for a bit with Charles," Paul said to Isaac. "I'll be back."

"I didn't see you there, Charles," Isaac said. "How are Sarah and the three babies, little Paul, Lewis, and John?"

"They are well, sir," Charles said. "They're gettin' big. And you and Mrs.

Griffin?"

"Doin' the best we can, son," Isaac said.

Paul and Charles went outside to speak in private.

"Pop, I'm taking Sarah and the babies to Kentucky," Charles blurted out. "Sarah's brother and me are gonna start our own flatboat building business and a ferry service across the Ohio River. Her brother's been down there already and says settlements are poppin' up everywhere. The Congress passed something called the Northwest Territory Ordinance of 1787, opening up a whole new area of the country. It covers the Ohio Valley from the Ohio River to the Great Lakes and all the way out west to the Illinois Territory."

"Sounds prosperous, son," Paul responded. "But your mother's not gonna be happy about this, Charles."

"I know, Pop, but this is a real opportunity," Charles continued. "I know the boat buildin' business and Sarah's brother can help me. He's got a place picked out by the river. All we gotta do is get workin'. The time is ripe."

"I understand, but you know how attached your mother is to you," Paul explained. "You're her whole world, boy. She's goin' to be none too happy about you and your family leavin'. She never got over losin' William, you know."

"Yeah...Blue Jacket," Charles pondered. "I know. We'll be back to visit, though. It's not like I'm joinin' the Shawnee. I gotta get out on my own, Pop. It's time for me to make my own way. You and Isaac have a good business and I was glad to be a part of it. But that's yours and his. I want my own business and to make my own fortune."

"I understand, son," Paul said. "I'm proud of you. I know you're a good hard worker and you'll do well in your endeavor. I'm just worried about your mother."

Charles felt bad about leaving his mother, but he had made up his mind. Charles quickly changed the subject by talking about Blue Jacket.

"They say William...I mean Blue Jacket, is the chief of the Shawnee now, leadin' war parties all over Ohio," Charles revealed. "It's hard to believe he's my brother and the son of my dear sweet ma. It don't seem possible."

"I know, son," Paul said.

"It seems so strange a white man could fight with the Indians killin' other white folks," Charles said. "I never could get over how Jim Griffin just up and left with the Indians, leavin' his folks and everything. I thought Jim was my friend, too. I reckon he became a savage just like William. I'll never understand it, Pop. It just don't seem right."

"It don't," Paul said. "But they was just boys when the Shawnee took 'em. The Shawnee have a way of makin' boys feel like they're brave men. They have such great respect for courage and bravery that boys kind o' get tricked by 'em, I guess. It's sort o' like a girl gettin' told how pretty she is all the time. Sometimes it kind o' goes to their heads."

"Yeah, I reckon," Charles said. "I remember Jim could do anything. Maybe he liked them Injuns tellin' him all the time how great he was. Mr. Griffin wasn't never tellin' him that. But I'll still never understand how they can kill innocent white folks. There's plenty o' room for everybody. This here's a big country."

"I agree, son, but it was the Indians' land first," Paul responded.

# Chapter 12

In the autumn of that same year in northwest Ohio at Fort Jefferson, General Arthur St. Clair led a punitive expedition of more than one thousand regular United States Army troops and militia. Their goal was to rid the Indians from the Ohio Valley once and for all to make it safe for white settlers. Before dawn, the troops lined up in formation preparing to leave Fort Jefferson. General St. Clair, sitting high on his horse, led the procession of soldiers from the gates of Fort Jefferson. Most of the troops were on foot, while all of the officers were on horseback.

"General St. Clair, the regiments are ready to march," an officer declared.

"Very good, Major," the General responded. "Maybe we can eradicate these Indians from Ohio for good."

"Yes sir," the Major said.

"Give the order for the march, Major," the General directed.

"Troops, prepare for march," the Major shouted.

"Troops, prepare for march...march!" another officer echoed in the ranks.

The troops exited the fort in perfect formation, parading into the wilderness. As the troops marched along the Wabash River in western Ohio in pursuit of the Ohio Indian nations, members of the Shawnee, Miami, and Delaware tribes were encamped less than ten miles away. Chief Blue Jacket and Miami Chief Little Turtle were readying for battle in a large Indian camp consisting of two thousand Shawnee, Miami, and Delaware warriors. A Shawnee scout arrived in the Indians' camp a few hours later to report that the United States Army was approaching.

"Chief Blue Jacket, Chief Little Turtle, the soldiers are marching toward our camp on foot, maybe one thousand strong," the scout reported. "They will be here soon, long before the sun disappears."

"They will not get this far," Blue Jacket responded with supreme confidence.

Blue Jacket motioned to Chief Little Turtle and to his warriors, pointing in different directions, indicating his orders for battle. The Chiefs already had their battle plan in place. They were merely waiting for the soldiers to approach their position. Now that they determined they were indeed coming, the Shawnee, Miami, and the Delaware tribes were ready to implement their plan of attack. The Indian warriors organized quickly and left camp in preparation for a massive ambush on the soldiers.

At midday, General St. Clair's army marched through a valley only a few miles from the Indian camp. A thousand Indians rode on horseback over a hill on one side. Another thousand Indians rode over a hill on the other side, converging on St. Clair's troops in the valley. The Indians caught the soldiers by complete surprise. With the exception of a handful of officers on horseback, the soldiers were at an even greater disadvantage being on foot. The Indian warriors began killing the troops in what would amount to an all-out massacre. The sound of howling Indians, continuous gunfire, and men groaning in agony was heard throughout the countryside.

General St. Clair and his troops were completely vulnerable. The Indians had taken clear advantage with the element of surprise from higher ground. Chief Blue Jacket and Chief Little Turtle led a superior force of two thousand Shawnee, Delaware, and Miami Indians against General St. Clair's force of one thousand regular army and militia, ultimately killing six hundred troops and wounding four hundred in the worst defeat in history on the United States Army by American Indians. This was far worse than the more famous massacre of

Custer's Last Stand almost a century later in 1876 where three thousand Sioux and Cheyenne Indians killed General Custer and two hundred of his men at the Battle of Little Big Horn.

## *Chapter 13*

In December 1787 at the Apple Orchard farm, Alice had fallen ill.  She had been bed-ridden for days, and Paul was attentive to her every need.

"Take some of this good beef soup," Paul said.  "It will make you strong."

"I'm not hungry," Alice retorted, weak and tired from her illness.  She had aged beyond her years.

"Where is Charles?" she asked, somewhat confused.

"You know where he is, Alice," Paul answered.  "He's gone to Kentucky with his wife and sons.  He's got a ferry business takin' folks across the Ohio River.  He wrote last month, remember?  He's doing well and Sarah's gonna have another baby."

"Oh yes, I remember now," she said.  "I miss them.  I'm so proud of Charles.  He is such a good, hardworking, young man, and such a great father.  I'm so glad I managed to produce at least one child to live a normal life."

"When you get better, we'll take a canoe trip on the river to see them," Paul reassured her.  "Just like we did over twenty-five years ago, remember?"

"How could I ever forget?" she said. "We had quite an adventure, didn't we Paul? You saved me. I've had a good life with you, Paul. I wanted to die after the Indians killed George and my babies. You were the one that convinced me otherwise. I'm glad William never had to see his mother bein' burned at the stake. I hope he's still alive, even if he is a Shawnee."

"You just get some rest," Paul said. "You're goin' to be just fine."

"Paul, don't stay all alone in this house after I'm gone," Alice pleaded.

"Don't be ridiculous, Alice," Paul said. "You're not goin' nowhere."

"I love you, Paul," she said. "Maybe you can read to me from my Bible."

"I will," Paul said. "But first let's get some food into you."

Paul put his arm around the back of her neck to prop her up to feed her. He gently laid a napkin over her chest before dipping a spoon into the warm broth. But before he could bring the spoon to her lips, Alice's head suddenly fell to one side.

"Alice! Alice!" Paul shouted excitedly.

Paul placed his cheek against her mouth and nose to see if he could detect any breath. He started to panic when he felt no air stir against his face. He pressed his hand against her chest to feel for a heartbeat, but her heart had stopped. Realizing she had passed away, Paul wrapped his arms around her hugging her tightly and wept as he had never wept before in his life.

Days later at the Mount Moriah Presbyterian Church Cemetery in Springhill Township, a preacher stood over Alice's grave with a Bible in hand, having just concluded her funeral. Paul dropped dirt onto her coffin. Isaac and Mary were standing next to Paul. Several people stood around the grave. The tombstone was engraved:

ALICE LARSH
1730- 1787
REST IN PEACE

As Isaac placed his arm around Paul to comfort him, leading him away from the gravesite, the other attendees dispersed as well.

Charles did not attend the funeral. Charles, his pregnant wife, Sarah, and their three sons, Paul, age five, Lewis, age three, and John, age one, were all back home in Kentucky. Paul had written Charles a long letter describing his mother's passing and her funeral. He told Charles that his mother had spoken of him with love and pride in her last moments. The letter reached Charles two months later.

Charles was shattered at the news. He could not help but feel riddled with guilt at having not been there. He told Sarah over and over again how much he regretted the timing of their move to Kentucky. If only he had waited another year before leaving, he told her repeatedly, he would have had more time to spend with his mother. He beat himself up even more for missing her funeral. Charles began to wonder if he had been a good son. All of these thoughts, no matter how irrational, haunted him in his grief.

Charles had trouble for months getting over the death of his mother, continually contemplating and brooding over the decisions he made. His self-recrimination persisted. One day several months after his mother's death, Sarah finally had had enough of Charles' second-guessing his past.

"Charles Larsh," Sarah sternly said. "You have got to move on. I have heard enough of your maudlin attitude. You have nothing to feel guilty about. You brought your family to Kentucky for a better life. This is our path and it is meant to be."

"I reckon you're right," Charles said self-consciously.

"Of course I am," she said. "And don't you forget what your father wrote you. Your dear sweet departed mother did nothing but sing your praises. Her last words were about you and how much she loved you."

"I know, I know," Charles said.

"You were not only a wonderful son, but you are the best husband and father anybody could ask for," Sarah continued. "Our kin are goin' to die, Charles, regardless of where we go or what we do."

"I reckon so," Charles said again.

"Charles, we all must live in the moment and meet our loved ones in glory," she said.

Nine months later in the office of Larsh-Griffin Shipping in Wilson Point, Paul was discussing the state of his life with his friend Isaac. Paul, like his son, had a difficult time getting over the loss of Alice.

"Isaac," Paul said. "I need to talk to someone. I'm so damned lonely and depressed. I don't know what to do."

"I'm here for you, Paul," Isaac responded. "I wish you would talk to me. You've barely said three words to me since Alice passed away."

"I know and I'm sorry, Isaac," Paul said. "I've just been grievin' so. I miss Alice. We were as close as any two people could be, even after all the years we were married. I bet we shared more together and been through more than most folks could even imagine. I really don't know how I'm goin' to make it without her."

"You'll make it, Paul," Isaac said. "You're a survivor and a fighter."

"I'll be all right, I guess," Paul said. "I miss her though. I was used to being alone in my younger days. It never bothered me then, but I was young and ambitious. Now I'm older and have settled down in my ways. But I just can't stand it without her here. Since I rescued her that night from the Shawnee, we were never separated. Do you know it took her two and half years before she would marry me? I pestered her every single day before she said yes."

"Is that right?" Isaac said. "You never

told me that before."

"Yeah, I spent every day after that with her right up to the day she died," Paul said.

"You know Alice would want you to move on with your life and be happy," Isaac said.

"I know she would...I'll try," Paul said.

"You should come to the church social with Mary and me Saturday night," Isaac pleaded. "It would do you good. You've been cooped up too long in the house. It ain't healthy to be alone all the time."

"I know it ain't," Paul said. "You win, I'll come."

"Good," Isaac said. "I'm glad we talked."

"Me too," Paul said.

"I've got some news about Blue Jacket," Isaac said.

"What is it?" Paul asked. "Is he dead?"

"No, I wish he was though," Isaac said. "I saw a newspaper from Fort Pitt. Says Chief Blue Jacket of the Shawnee and Chief Little Turtle of the Miami led an Indian attack against the United States Army in Ohio killin' over six hundred soldiers and wounding another four hundred. The Injuns only lost fifty."

"That's awful," Paul said, shaking his head in disgust.

"I shoulda' killed him that day when I had the chance," Isaac said.

"They woulda' killed Jim, though," Paul said.

"Maybe six hundred soldiers wouldn't be dead now," Isaac responded. "Jim was probably with them savages, if he's still alive. We coulda' prevented all of it."

"Killin' one man wouldna' stopped the Shawnee," Paul told Isaac as he put his arm around him to console him.

A week later, Paul accompanied Isaac and Mary to the Mount Moriah Presbyterian Church hall to the dance. A fiddler was playing music. A man was calling out square dancing instructions. Paul was standing with Isaac and Mary, drinking punch and watching the festivities. An attractive thirty-four-year-old woman named Elizabeth Johnson approached them.

"Good evenin', Mary, Isaac," she said.

"Good evenin', Elizabeth," Isaac said.

"Good evenin', Elizabeth," Mary said. "Do

you know Paul Larsh?"

"Yes, I know of him, but we've never had the pleasure of bein' properly introduced."

"Paul, this is Elizabeth Johnson," Mary said. "Her husband, Tom Johnson, passed on suddenly last year."

"Oh yes, I met Mr. Johnson," Paul said. "He had some business with us. I had no idea he had passed on. I'm sorry to hear of your loss, ma'am. Mr. Johnson was an honest and agreeable man to conduct business with."

"Thank you, Mr. Larsh, for saying so," Elizabeth said. "Although I never met Mrs. Larsh, I was saddened to hear of her passing."

"Yes, death is inevitable, I guess," Paul said. "My wise friend Isaac here tells me that the livin' have to keep toilin' through it all. I'm tryin' to follow his advice."

"Well, then maybe you'll do me the honor of dancin' with me," she boldly requested.

Paul said sheepishly, "I've never been much for dancin', but I'll give it a try."

Paul and Elizabeth jumped into the line for square dancing. Elizabeth danced happily with all smiles. Paul danced a bit ungracefully at

first, but he knew all of the steps. He and
Elizabeth were soon smiling at one another.
They had an immediate attraction despite their
considerable age difference. Paul was fifty-
four years old, but physically fit. He had a
full head of thick, wavy hair, mostly brown in
color, but with some graying. His face was
lined, but he still possessed the rugged,
handsome, good looks of his younger years.

Paul and Elizabeth had only a brief
courtship before deciding to get married.
Elizabeth was very eager to start a family. At
thirty-four years old, she believed she could
not wait any longer to have children. Her
marriage to her first husband was a good
marriage, but Elizabeth always felt unfulfilled
at not bearing any children. She discussed her
dreams of having babies with Paul. He agreed
that they should not wait and made their
engagement very short.

The wedding took place at the Mount Moriah
Presbyterian Church, just a few months following
their meeting at the square dance. Isaac was
the best man, and his wife, Mary, was the matron
of honor. Only a small group of people, some
neighbors and friends from the church, attended
the ceremony. Charles and his young family were
not there, as they could not make the trip from
Kentucky. Charles also could not leave his

bustling ferry and shipping business.

Within a year and a half, Elizabeth was expecting a baby.  When she went into labor, her good friend, Mary Griffin, was there to help with the delivery.  Paul and Isaac helped too, bringing hot water and blankets into her bedroom.

"You men wait out there," Mary told Isaac and Paul as they lingered in the bedroom.

Paul and Isaac obeyed and left immediately. Mary closed the door behind them.

"I'm way too old for this," Paul said anxiously.

"You're doing fine," Isaac told him.

"It's been thirty years since Charles was born in Kaskaskia," Paul said emotively. "Fifty-six-year-old men should not be having babies.  I'm a grandfather for cryin' out loud!"

"This is unusual," Isaac responded. "Charles' baby brother or sister will be thirty years younger than he is!  And Charles' children are goin' to have an aunt or an uncle younger than them.  Imagine that!"

"I remember Alice had Charles so quickly," Paul continued.  "I thought she was born for

makin' babies.  We never had another though.  I
don't know why.  It just never happened.  Wasn't
for a lack of tryin'.  I guess the good Lord
just blessed us with Charles and that was it."

"I envy you, Paul," Isaac said.  "I used to
think the same thing about Jim."

"I'm sorry, Isaac," Paul said after
realizing he might have been insensitive.  "I
know you and Mary miss your Jim."

"It's all right, Paul," Isaac told him.
"I'm happy for you."

"I've been thinking, Isaac, ever since
Elizabeth told me she was expecting this baby, I
want you to buy out my share of the business.
I'm gettin' too old and tired for farmin' and
operatin' the shipping business too.  I need to
spend time with Elizabeth and this new baby now
more than ever.  I can't believe I have all that
much time left here on this earth anyway."

"Yes, Paul," Isaac said.  "I understand
completely.  I've had many the same thoughts.
I'm too old for all this work too.  Maybe we'll
just sell the whole damn thing."

At that moment, a baby was heard crying in
the bedroom.  Paul and Isaac stopped their
conversation abruptly.  Mary opened the bedroom
door and motioned for Paul and Isaac to enter.

Paul eagerly rushed through the door with Isaac following.

"You have a beautiful, healthy daughter," Mary said to Paul.

Paul knelt at Elizabeth's bedside. Elizabeth was holding her new baby, alternately smiling at her newborn baby in her arms and at Paul.

"Meet your baby girl," she told him. "I'm going to call her Hannah after my mother."

"She's got your eyes," Paul lovingly told Elizabeth.

"I'm so happy," she said, looking at Paul affectionately.

# Chapter 14

Two years later, Paul met with his lawyer, James Hughes, in Springhill Township. Isaac accompanied Paul to Hughes' office in the middle of town where a shingle hung outside the door, "James Hughes - Attorney at Law."

"Good mornin', Mr. Hughes," Paul said as he and Isaac entered the office.

"Good mornin', Mr. Larsh, I've been expecting you," Hughes said.

"You know Isaac Griffin, don't you?" Paul asked.

"Yes, of course," Hughes said. "How are you Mr. Griffin?"

"I'm very well, thank you," Isaac said. "Good to see you again, Mr. Hughes."

"I've finished drafting your will, Mr. Larsh, per your instructions," Hughes said.

"That's fine, Mr. Hughes," Paul said.

"I'll read it aloud," Hughes said. "In the name of God. Amen. I, Paul Larsh, of the County of Fayette in the Commonwealth of Pennsylvania, being of sound mind and body, thanks be to God, calling to mind the mortality of all flesh and that it is appointed for all men once to die, do on this seventeenth day of November in the year of our Lord, one thousand seven hundred and ninety-two, publish this my last will and testament in the name and way following. First and principally, I recommend my soul to God that gave it and my body to the dust, nothing doubting but that I shall receive the same again at the general resurrection of all flesh according to the mighty power of God and his touching of my temporal estate with which it has pleased God to bless me with, I will and bequeath it in the way and manner following after funeral expenses, and I allow all my just debts to be paid also. I will bequeath to my beloved wife, Elizabeth, her wearing apparel, her choice of all my beds and furniture, there to also her choice of all the horses, her saddle and bridle, three cows to be chosen likewise by herself, all the stock of sheep, a set of tea ware, six pewter plates, also two basins and two pots, the one-third of the land on which I now live, during her widowhood which must include the house I now live in and fifty acres of clear land adjoining thereto, and privilege of firewood and necessary timber from any part of said plantation. Secondly, I bequeath to my son, Charles Larsh, the one third of said plantation, my wearing apparel, a King James Bible, and a rifle given to him and his heirs forever. Thirdly, I bequeath to my daughter, Hannah, one third of the aforesaid plantation to her and her heirs forever and it is my will and request that the residue of my moveable estate be sold by my executors thereafter named at Vendue (a public sale at auction) and the sum arising from said sale together with what may be in due me be equally divided between my wife and children, Charles and Hannah, which third part of my land I now live on and of my personal estate by this will bequeathed to my wife shall be in lieu of her dower and after the marriage or death of my wife Elizabeth, I will and bequeath to my children the land I bequeathed to her to be equally divided between them my said children and their heirs forever, and should the Almighty God bless us with more children, it is my will that they be made equal sharers of my estate notwithstanding the former bequeathments, and it is my further will and testament that my well beloved wife, Elizabeth, and my beloved son, Charles Larsh, and my worthy friend Isaac Griffin, to be the whole and sole Executors of this my last will and testament hereby revoking and renouncing of all former wills, gifts, and legacies, confirming this and no other to be my last will and testament in testimony whereof I have hereto set my hand and seal this seventeenth day of November in the year of our Lord one thousand seven hundred and ninety-two."

Hughes lowered his head a bit in order to

see over his reading glasses at Paul for his approval.

"It sounds as if you've covered everything, Mr. Hughes," Paul said.

"I hope it proves satisfactory to you," Hughes added.

"It does," Paul responded.

Hughes pushed the document in front of Paul pointing to the place where he needed to sign. Paul signed the will. Hughes slid the will in front of Isaac indicating where he should sign.

"Mr. Griffin, sign here as a witness," Hughes directed him.

Isaac signed the will. Hughes put his signature on the document and notarized it.

"There, I'm glad that's taken care of," Paul said gratefully. "Thank you, Isaac. Thank you, Mr. Hughes."

"You're welcome, Paul," Isaac said as he nodded to Paul, acknowledging his gratitude.

"You're welcome, Mr. Larsh," Hughes responded.

Paul and Isaac shook hands with Hughes and departed his office.

"It's a strange feeling to be all ready to die," Paul said to Isaac as they walked to their wagon.

"Don't be ridiculous, Paul," Isaac responded.

"Nobody lives forever," Paul said bluntly.

"I reckon not," Isaac said.

# Chapter 15

For the next year and a half, Paul devoted his life entirely to Elizabeth and their daughter, Hannah.  One sunny spring afternoon in 1794, Paul was playing with Hannah, now four years old, in front of their farmhouse at Apple Orchard.  Elizabeth sat on the front porch watching them.  She had never been happier, so pleased with her tranquil life.  Elizabeth had finally realized her dream of having a family.  She felt an even greater appreciation for life as she and Paul awaited the arrival of their second child.  Paul was a loving, devoted husband, and Hannah, their beautiful daughter, was the joy of their life.

It was not as if her former husband, Tom Johnson, had not been every bit as dedicated as Paul.  She possessed nothing but fond memories of Tom, but the only thing missing in her relationship with him was a family.  Elizabeth never told Tom, but it always saddened her.  Elizabeth now had everything she ever wanted.

Suddenly, just as she was feeling so blessed, Paul clutched his chest wincing in pain.  He looked to Elizabeth for help, not wanting Hannah to see him suffering.  Elizabeth ran to his aid, seeing the panic-stricken expression on Paul's face.  Paul dropped to one knee, grasping each arm with the opposite hand.

Elizabeth gripped Paul under his shoulder helping him up. By this time, his face turned white. She managed to help him slowly stagger into the house. They barely made it into the bedroom where Paul finally fell like a log on the bed, his legs dangling off the side. After she lifted his legs onto the bed, she pulled a blanket over him to make him more comfortable.

"Oh, Paul...you'll be all right, you have to be," she said as she hugged him.

At that very moment, Paul said with his last breath, "I'm sorry, Elizabeth." His head drooped as he passed away in her arms. She buried her head into his chest, weeping uncontrollably.

Paul's funeral was held two days later at the Mount Moriah Presbyterian Church. A crowd was gathered around Paul's grave at the cemetery. The same preacher from Alice's funeral was presiding. Elizabeth, Hannah, Isaac, Mary, and Charles were there, along with several other friends from the community. Charles just happened to be en route to Pennsylvania to visit his father and meet his stepmother and half-sister for the very first time. Charles arrived the day after his father died. His wife, Sarah, and their seven children, aged one month to twelve years, stayed behind in Kentucky, unable to make such a long and demanding trip across the wilderness.

The preacher addressed the mourners saying, "Please bow your heads."

He calmly turned the pages of the Bible to get to the appropriate passage. He read, "From James, chapter four, verse fourteen: Whereas ye know not what shall be on the morrow. For what is your life? It is even a vapour, that appeareth for a little time, and then vanisheth away."

The preacher paused before turning the pages of the Bible again. By pure coincidence, the preacher recited the very same prophetic passage Alice read to Paul thirty-eight years before on their first trip down the river.

"For every thing there is a season, and a time for every purpose under the heaven: A time to be born, and a time to die; A time to plant, and a time to pluck up that which is planted; A time to kill, and a time to heal; a time to break down, and a time to build up; A time to weep, and a time to laugh; a time to mourn, and a time to dance. Ecclesiastes, chapter three, verses one through four," he said.

The preacher concluded, "We give thee, Oh Lord, to your great and tender mercy, this simple God-fearing man, Paul Larsh, who loved and provided for his wife and children, was loyal to his friends, and was respected by all who knew him.  Have mercy on his soul.  Amen."

"Amen," the crowd said in unison.

Holding Hannah in one hand, Elizabeth clenched a handful of dirt, releasing it from her hand and watching it fall atop the pine casket, deep in his grave.  She walked away with tears streaming down her face, thoroughly disillusioned at how her perfect life with Paul had ended so abruptly.

The mourners moved away from the burial site, revealing his tombstone next to Alice Larsh's, engraved:

PAUL LARSH
DEPARTED THIS LIFE ANNO DOMINI 1794
A GOOD CITIZEN A LOVING HUSBAND
AND TENDER PARENT

Charles stayed with his stepmother and half-sister for as long as he could, but his family and business were waiting for him back in Kentucky.  He tried to convince Elizabeth to bring Hannah and join his family there, but she was unwilling to leave her home and the resting place of the man she had loved so dearly. Elizabeth raised her children and lived out her life at Apple Orchard, never marrying again.

The aforementioned story of Paul L'Archevêque was based on real-life events. Historical evidence and family histories concerning Paul L'Archevêque were used as the basis for writing this novel. The Indian massacre in 1756 at Jackson River, Augusta County, Virginia, killing George Kincaid and thirteen others, truly happened. Mrs. Kincaid and her three children were actually taken prisoner by the Shawnee Indians.

Descriptions of Paul L'Archevêque's daring rescue of Alice Dean Kincaid from the Shawnee Indians were discovered in family histories. Documented records revealed that Paul L'Archevêque and Alice Dean Kincaid were married on June 19, 1759 at the Church of St. Anne's at Fort Chartres in the French settlement of Kaskaskia, Illinois. Family histories also disclosed that Paul and Alice found it necessary to escape Kaskaskia after Paul assaulted a priest by hurling him into a fire in retaliation for the priest burning Alice's Protestant Bible. Paul Larsh's Last Will and Testament was taken virtually word for word from his original will, recorded in Fayette County, Pennsylvania, on November 17, 1792.

The revenge on white settlers by the Shawnee Indians in the late 1750s in Maryland,

Pennsylvania, and Virginia was a historical fact.  Following General Edward Braddock's crushing defeat by the French and Indians just south of Fort Duquesne in July 1755, a delegation of Shawnee and Delaware Indians protesting the loss of their land was indeed hanged in Philadelphia.  No Shawnee or Delaware Indians participated in the battle at Fort Duquesne in 1755.

The details concerning the history of the French and Indian War were researched thoroughly and described as accurately as possible.

Chief Black Hoof was a real Shawnee Indian chief who lived in the Ohio Valley during the 1700s.  Little information was known regarding his early life or his date of birth.  His date of birth was reported by different sources to have been from 1719 to 1740.  It was more likely he was born closer to 1740, since he was known to have died in Ohio in 1831 shortly after signing a treaty ceding the last of the Shawnee lands in Ohio to the United States.  He was probably closer to ninety-one years old when he died than one hundred and twelve years old.

During the French and Indian War, Chief Black Hoof had been allied with the French.  He was believed to have taken part in many battles throughout his life, including the massacre of General St. Clair's army.  He was purported to have taken one hundred and twenty-seven scalps during his lifetime as a Shawnee Indian warrior. It was not known if Paul L'Archevêque ever traded with Chief Black Hoof personally, or if he actually rescued Alice Kincaid from Chief Black Hoof himself; however, it was quite possible that Paul L'Archevêque might have come in contact with Chief Black Hoof at some point during his fur trading days in the Ohio Valley.

The true story of Blue Jacket, another real Shawnee Indian chief in the late 1700s, was changed slightly in this novel for the purposes of better storytelling. Chief Blue Jacket was reported to have been the brother of Charles Larsh's wife, Sarah Van Swearingen, according to various family histories. The Shawnee Indians supposedly captured Sarah's brother, Marmaduke Van Swearingen, at an early age. He was believed to have been raised by the Shawnee and later became known as Chief Blue Jacket. However, Shawnee descendants of Blue Jacket have refuted this assertion and claim Blue Jacket was not born a white man at all. Chief Blue Jacket fought alongside Miami Chief Little Turtle in several battles against the United States Army, including the General St. Clair massacre. Chief Blue Jacket's date of birth was reported to be around 1745. He died in approximately 1810.

Chief Blue Jacket's name appeared as a

signatory on two Indian treaties with the United States. The first treaty Chief Blue Jacket signed was the Treaty of Greenville after losing the Battle of Fallen Timbers in 1794. On August 20, 1794, General Anthony Wayne led United States Army troops to defeat Shawnee and Miami warriors in Ohio, which later became known as the Battle of Fallen Timbers, the last major battle fought by Chief Blue Jacket and Chief Little Turtle. A year later, on August 3, 1795, at Fort Greenville, Ohio, Chief Blue Jacket, Chief Little Turtle, and other Indian leaders signed the Greenville Treaty, surrendering most of their land to the United States, thereby opening more areas of Ohio to white settlers.

Chief Blue Jacket's signature appeared again on the Treaty of Fort Industry in 1805. This treaty was a successor to the Greenville Treaty, relinquishing more than a half million acres of Indian lands in northeastern Ohio to the United States. Chief Blue Jacket and Chief Black Hoof both signed the Treaty of Fort Industry on July 4, 1805. Representatives from the Delaware and other tribes also signed the Treaty of Fort Industry. However, neither Chief Little Turtle nor any other member of the Miami tribe signed this treaty.

The massacre of General Arthur St. Clair's army in Ohio by the Shawnee, Miami, and the

Delaware tribes, led by Chief Blue Jacket and Miami Chief Little Turtle, actually occurred in 1791, four years later than depicted in this novel. The date was changed to fit the storyline of the novel. In fact, the massacre was the worst defeat ever inflicted upon the United States Army by American Indians. Although the outcome of the massacre and the casualty totals were represented as accurately as possible, the details of the battle were not described exactly as they occurred. In the actual battle, the Shawnee, Miami, and Delaware Indian warriors accomplished their surprise attack on General St. Clair's army encampment near the Wabash River in western Ohio in the frigid early morning hours of November 4, 1791, killing six hundred army troops and wounding another four hundred.

Paul Larsh's second wife, Elizabeth Larsh, was not known to have ever remarried. She possibly lived out her days on the Apple Orchard farm in Springhill Township, Fayette County, Pennsylvania. It was determined through court records that Elizabeth Larsh had been pregnant at the time of Paul's death. She bore a posthumous son, John Larsh, who was entitled to an equal share of his father's estate. However, John died before reaching one year of age. Following John's death, Charles Larsh filed a lawsuit against his half-sister, Hannah, arguing that John's share of their father's estate should be equally divided between him and Hannah, as survivors. The attorney for the defendant argued that Hannah, John's full-blooded sister, should inherit John's share of the estate. In September 1796, the court ruled in Charles' favor as follows, "the son, John, having died intestate, in his minority, unmarried, and without issue, the estate descending to him from his father is to be equally divided among the surviving children of his father."

No further details concerning the remainder of Elizabeth Larsh's life or her death could be determined. More information was known regarding Paul and Elizabeth Larsh's daughter, Hannah Larsh. She married George Gans in 1808 in Fayette County, Pennsylvania, and bore eight children. George Gans died in 1825 at the age of forty-two. In that same year, Hannah married Joseph Baker, thirteen years her junior. She had four children with Joseph.

On February 28, 1850, Hannah and Joseph Baker signed an indenture selling land from Paul Larsh's original three hundred and seventy acre farm, Apple Orchard, to her eight children from her previous marriage at a cost of one dollar per child. The sale did not include the approximately one hundred and thirty acres on which Hannah and Joseph currently lived.  It also did not include the ninety-six acres Charles Larsh inherited.  The indenture indicated that Philip Dilz owned the ninety-six acres previously owned by Charles Larsh, deeded to him from the executor of George Kramer, deceased, as recorded in the Recorder's Office, March 8, 1816.

Family histories revealed that Joseph Baker died in 1858 at the age of fifty-five.  Hannah Larsh Baker died on February 2, 1872 in Uniontown, Fayette County, Pennsylvania.  She was buried at the Mount Moriah Baptist Cemetery in Smithfield, Pennsylvania.

Charles Larsh apparently sold his one-third inheritance from his father's farm based on the details in the aforementioned indenture.  The indenture did not indicate when Charles sold the land or to whom.  It only revealed the identities of the last two owners of the land Charles inherited.  The lawsuit he brought against his half-sister, however, may have been precipitated by his desire to sell his share of the estate.  After his half-brother, John Larsh, was born, Charles' inheritance decreased from owning one-third of his family farm to less than a fourth.  Following John's death, the court ruling in Charles' favor reverted his share of the inheritance back to the original one-third entitlement.

Evidence suggested he returned to his family in Kentucky where he and his sons prospered. Charles and Sarah Larsh had a total of twelve children, according to records from the Church of Jesus Christ of Latter Day Saints and United States Census records. Five of their children were born in Pennsylvania from 1782 to 1789, while the remaining seven were reportedly born in Kentucky from 1790 to 1799.

Family histories indicated that Charles Larsh's family lived in Maysville, Kentucky, on the Ohio River for many years, building flatboats and operating a ferry. Charles Larsh and his sons reportedly completed many trips shipping various goods on flatboats to New Orleans, Louisiana, via the Ohio and Mississippi Rivers. Charles Larsh was believed to have died around 1815 in Kentucky. His wife and some of their children eventually resettled north in Dixon Township, Preble County, Ohio, according to United States Census records. Sarah Larsh died on March 14, 1849 at the age of eighty-eight. She was buried in the Harris Cemetery in Dixon Township, Preble County, Ohio.

Charles and Sarah Larsh's oldest son, Paul Larsh, born in 1782 in Fayette County, Pennsylvania, lived a very eventful life on the American frontier in the nineteenth century, much the same as his namesake grandfather had during the eighteenth century. A biographical sketch of Colonel Paul Larsh appeared in the *Eaton Register* newspaper on March 12, 1875. John Charles Larsh authored the article, however, his exact familial relationship to Colonel Paul Larsh was uncertain. Much of the following information was derived from this newspaper article.

Paul Larsh met his wife during the summer of 1806 on a trip from his home in Kentucky through the wilderness to visit the place of his birth in Fayette County, Pennsylvania. After stopping at a relative's home to rest in Pennsylvania, he met Miss Mercy Minor, daughter of General John Minor of Green County, Pennsylvania. They later married on November 6, 1806. Within a few days after their marriage, they travelled west back to Kentucky on horseback, arriving at his father's residence on the Ohio River in early December 1806. Paul Larsh and Mercy Minor had eleven children surviving to adulthood from 1807 to 1827, and a twelfth child who died in infancy in 1825.

Paul Larsh purchased a tract of farmland in Dixon Township, Preble County, Ohio, in 1809 and settled there with his wife and family. Within a short time in the coming years, Paul Larsh was appointed Assessor of Preble County. In 1812, he was elected Sheriff of Preble County, only the second Sheriff ever elected by the county. He served two years and was succeeded by Samuel Ward for four years. Paul Larsh was elected Sheriff of Preble County again in 1818 and re-elected in 1820, serving six years in total.

During the War of 1812, Paul Larsh served as a Quartermaster in charge of supplies for Fort Nisbet, Fort Black, and Fort Greenville in Ohio. During his service, it was reported that a camp of friendly Shawnee Indians wintered not far from his homestead, providing protection to his family from any hostile Indians during his absence. His service during the War of 1812 most likely accounted for his break in service as Sheriff of Preble County from 1814 to 1818. However, he was elected Justice of the Peace of Dixon Township, as well as Captain of the Militia during those years. He was later elected as Colonel of his regiment in Dixon Township.

On January 1, 1819, Sheriff Paul Larsh moved to Eaton Township, Preble County, Ohio, for three years. On January 1, 1822, he returned to his farm in Dixon Township. In 1829, he moved his family to a farm in Wayne County, near Richmond, Indiana. In 1833, he moved again after purchasing a tract of land near the Whitewater River, south of Richmond. He built a flourmill on a tributary of the Whitewater River and prospered.

In 1867, Colonel Paul Larsh, at the age of eighty-four, traveled to Illinois to sell a tract of land he owned. He had planned to purchase another tract of land near Kaskaskia, Illinois, once owned by his grandfather. Before he could transact any business, however, he died of cholera on August 13, 1867. He was buried near Kaskaskia, Illinois, the former residence of his grandfather, Paul L'Archevêque, and the birthplace of his father, Charles Larsh.

The biographical sketch in the *Eaton Register* in 1875 described Colonel Paul Larsh's physical appearance as "a remarkably symmetrically built, well-proportioned man, 5 ft. 10 inches high, compactly knit, and weighing, when in the prime of his life about one hundred and seventy-five pounds. He was very athletic, active, and hardy – capable of undergoing almost any amount of fatigue, and was always first choice at a log rolling. His complexion was fair, hair light, and uncommonly fine bright blue eyes."

The article further described his mental faculties stating "...he was notable for strong, sound common sense, ready perception, remarkable retentive memory, logical, comprehensive, and rapid in his deductions. He was extremely social in disposition, fond of society and conversation, and sagacious in his judgment of men."

This newspaper article depicted Colonel Paul Larsh as a pioneer of America and a hero, not unlike his grandfather, Paul L'Archevêque, the character portrayed in this novel. The author of the newspaper article, John Charles Larsh, in his concluding line wrote, "Take the large majority of the young men of this day, and place them in the condition of those pioneers, and require them to accomplish similar results, and they would perish by the thousand like the stubble before the driving flame, in the face of the dangers and privations in their road." His summation was rather cynical and downright harsh with regard to the young men of his day. It seemed quite probable that in John Charles Larsh's opinion, no generation would have ever lived up to the hardships endured by the early American pioneers, and rightly so.

Colonel Paul Larsh and his wife Mercy's seventh child, Lewis W. Larsh, was born on February 19, 1819 in Preble County, Ohio. He married Mary V. Tackett of Ohio on March 7, 1841 in Richmond, Indiana. They had a total of thirteen children from 1842 to 1863, one of whom died in early childhood.

By 1850, according to United States Census records, Lewis W. Larsh and Mary V. (Tackett) Larsh were living on a farm in Peoria, Illinois, with seven children. Marenus Larsh was listed as the oldest at eight years old, and born in Indiana. (Marenus was spelled incorrectly in the United States Census records, as was the case with many names written in the United States Census. "Mirenus" was the correct spelling.) Five of Lewis W. Larsh and Mary V. Larsh's children were listed as born in Indiana, while the two youngest were listed as born in Illinois.

By 1860, the United States Census records indicated that Lewis W. Larsh and Mary Larsh were living on a farm in Des Moines Township, Polk County, Iowa, with eleven children. Lewis W. Larsh was listed as a farm laborer in 1860. Their five oldest children were listed as born in Indiana. The next four were born in Illinois, while the two youngest were born in Iowa, including Eddie W. Larsh, age one.

By 1870, the United States Census records revealed that the family of Lewis W. Larsh and Mary Larsh was residing in the Second Ward of

Des Moines, Polk County, Iowa. Only four children were living with them. Eddie W. Larsh had apparently died, as he was not listed in the 1870 United States Census. Two more children had been born in Iowa, Lincoln A. Larsh, age nine, and Lenney E. Larsh, age seven. Lewis W. Larsh's occupation was listed as turner. In the 1800s, a turner worked with wood on a lathe.

The 1880 United States Census listed Lewis W. Larsh and Mary Larsh residing in the Seventh Ward of Des Moines, Polk County, Iowa. Only one child was residing with them, their seventeen-year-old son, E. L. Larsh. His full true name was Leonard Ellsworth Larsh. Leonard was the only remaining offspring residing with Lewis W. Larsh and Mary Larsh by 1880, as all of the older children had apparently moved on to either marry or to be on their own. Lewis W. Larsh's occupation was listed as wood turner, Mary's as keeping house, and Leonard's as lather. A lather in the early twentieth century worked on the installation of ceilings or walls in the construction of buildings or structures. The job description for a lather working in the late nineteenth century, however, might possibly have been different.

The 1890 United States Census was not available inasmuch as those records were lost in a fire in 1921 in the basement of the Department of Commerce in Washington, D.C. where they were being stored. The *Des Moines City Directory, 1889-1891*, revealed Lewis W. Larsh residing at 116 E. Locust Street, occupation: wood turner. The *Omaha, Nebraska City Directory, 1889-1890*, revealed Leonard E. Larsh boarding at 406 N. 16th Street, occupation: lather. The 1895 Iowa State Census listed Lewis W. Larsh, age seventy-six, still residing in Des Moines.

The 1900 United States Census revealed Leonard Larsh, age thirty-seven, renting a home at 3127 Union Avenue, Chicago, Illinois. The records indicated that his wife, Amanda Larsh, age thirty-four, immigrated to the United States from Sweden in 1883. Amanda Larsh was listed as the mother of eight children, five now living, and married for nine years. The youngest, Mary Larsh, was listed as one year of age. Luletia Larsh was listed as age two, Lincoln Larsh, age three, Edgar Larsh, age five, and the eldest, Edith Larsh, as age seven. Leonard Larsh's mother, Mary Larsh, age eighty, born in Ohio, was residing with them. The 1900 United States Census erroneously listed Mary Larsh as widowed.

The 1900 United States Census revealed that Lewis W. Larsh was residing with his eldest son, Mirenus Larsh, in Des Moines, Iowa. Lewis W. Larsh was listed as divorced. Mary Larsh was therefore not widowed. Mary Larsh might possibly have been embarrassed to reveal to the United States Census taker that she was divorced and instead told him she was widowed. Unlike today's world, divorce was neither socially nor religiously acceptable in the year 1900.

Lewis W. Larsh died in 1901 and was buried in the Woodland Cemetery in Des Moines, Iowa. Mary (Tackett) Larsh later died in 1903 and was buried alongside her ex-husband. Their son, Mirenus F. Larsh, born March 20, 1842 in Wayne County, Indiana, and died June 4, 1930 in Des Moines, Iowa, was buried with his wife and parents in the family plot in the Woodland Cemetery.

In the 1910 United States Census, records revealed that Leonard E. Larsh and his family were residing at 1925 Herbert Street, Baltimore, Maryland. His occupation was listed as a mechanic and lather. The records indicated that his wife, Amanda C. Larsh, obtained her United States Citizenship in 1884. They had been married for nineteen years. The 1910 United States Census listed Leonard E. Larsh and Amanda C. Larsh as now having only four children, as opposed to the previous 1900 United States Census where five children were listed. The youngest child, Mary Larsh, who was listed in the previous 1900 United States Census as one year of age, was no longer listed. Her omission from the 1910 United States Census suggested that she died within the last ten years.

The eldest child, Edith Larsh, age sixteen, was listed in the 1910 United States Census as having had no school in the last year. The second eldest, Edgar Larsh, age fifteen, was also listed as having had no school in the last year. Edgar Larsh was listed as lather by occupation. Lincoln A. Larsh, age thirteen, was listed as deaf and dumb. The youngest child, age twelve, was now listed as Lolita Larsh, not "Luletia," as she was listed in the previous 1900 United States Census.

According to United States military records obtained from the National Archives, Edgar Larsh, born October 28, 1894, enlisted in the United States Navy August 25, 1913, and served for almost seven years until his Honorable Discharge on July 21, 1920. He reached the rank of Gunner's Mate First Class and was listed as a qualified diver. Edgar Larsh completely lost his hearing later in life, which was widely believed to be a direct result of his deep-sea diving duties in the United States Navy. In World War I, he was stationed at a United States Naval Base in Inverness, Scotland, as a Mine Inspector in the Mine Assembly Shop. The United States Navy was responsible for installing mines in the waters around Inverness during World War

I.  After the war ended, Edgar Larsh continued his Naval assignment, defusing and removing the mines.

It was during this time that Edgar Larsh met and fell in love with Elizabeth "Bessie" Chisholm, the youngest of four daughters of Alpin Chisholm, a former police constable in Inverness, and Elizabeth MacDougall Chisholm. Alpin Chisholm was apparently not at all pleased about his daughter's relationship with an American sailor.  According to family stories from Scottish relatives, Alpin Chisholm had previously disowned his eldest and only son, Duncan Chisholm, who evidently married against his father's wishes.  Family members speculated that Duncan Chisholm might have later immigrated to Canada with his new wife.

One could only imagine that Alpin Chisholm must have been greatly relieved when the American seaman, Edgar Larsh, sailed away from Scotland in 1919 aboard the U.S.S. Melville to his new assignment with the United States Navy in San Diego, California.  In 1920, Edgar Larsh was honorably discharged from the United States Navy and apparently still smitten with Bessie Chisholm.

Edgar Larsh returned to Inverness, Scotland, and secretly married Bessie Chisholm on April 25, 1921.  A copy of their marriage license revealed that they obtained a Sheriff's Warrant in Inverness for an immediate wedding, avoiding the usual two-week wait for a normal marriage license. According to Scottish relatives, Bessie Chisholm had been engaged to a solicitor in Inverness at the time of her elopement to Edgar Larsh. She reportedly left her family a note before leaving for the United States with her new husband immediately following her marriage. The note supposedly read, "By the time you read this letter, I will already be married and on a ship to America."

Edgar Larsh and Bessie Larsh raised three children in a rented row house at 1103 Federal Street in Baltimore, Maryland. All three children were born at home. Betty Amanda Larsh was born December 11, 1921. Lolita Margaret Larsh was born December 29, 1923. Edgar Alpine Larsh, the youngest, was born February 21, 1925. Edgar Alpine Larsh was nicknamed "Boy" which his parents and sisters called him throughout his entire life. His middle name was after his maternal grandfather, Alpin Chisholm. Either his mother, or whoever might have filled out his birth certificate, misspelled Alpin incorrectly by adding an e. He would always hate his middle name "Alpine" and joked that his mother must have been drunk when she named him. To my knowledge, he never revealed his middle name to anyone outside the family.

Edgar Alpine Larsh grew up during the Great Depression of the 1930s.  According to the 1930 United States Census, his paternal grandparents were also residing at 1103 Federal Street.  His grandmother, Amanda Larsh, died in 1936.  His grandfather, Leonard Larsh, died two years later in 1938.  Leonard and Amanda Larsh were buried in the Moreland Memorial Park Cemetery in Baltimore, Maryland, sadly without tombstones or any type of markers for their graves.  The family undoubtedly could not afford headstones during those hard times.

Edgar Alpine Larsh graduated from Baltimore Polytechnic Institute in 1942, excelling in all areas of study, particularly in mathematics. Upon graduation from high school, Edgar and his young patriotic friends were anxious to join the fight against the Nazis and Japanese in World War II.  They immediately volunteered to join the United States Marine Corps.  However, Edgar was only seventeen years old.  Being underage, he could not join any branch of the military without parental consent.  His father refused to sign the enlistment papers for the Marine Corps. Ever the proud Naval veteran, his father would only sign for him to join the Navy.

Thus, Edgar Alpine Larsh joined the United States Navy at the tender age of seventeen with his father's written consent.  The United States

Navy ironically misspelled his hated middle name, making it "Aldine." Every document of his Naval record, including his enlistment papers, his dog tags, every official assignment, every roster, and even his Honorable Discharge papers, incorrectly listed his name as Edgar Aldine Larsh.

Edgar served on the U.S.S. Detroit in the Pacific in World War II. He was a Signalman First Class on the cruiser. During General Quarters, Edgar's battle station was relief gunner on a twenty-millimeter cannon. The U.S.S. Detroit was part of a fleet of fifteen destroyers and three cruisers. His ship was equipped with radar for anti-submarine warfare. When a submarine was spotted, the U.S.S. Detroit would proceed to that area and drop depth charges. His ship was accidently damaged twice from depth charges from other ships in his own fleet. He also witnessed a torpedo from the American fleet that just missed his ship. The U.S.S. Detroit and the other ships in the fleet bombed the Aleutian Islands near Alaska in 1943. The Japanese attacked and occupied the islands in 1942. After the bombardment and assault, the Americans landed on the islands only to determine that the Japanese army had secretly evacuated.

While on the U.S.S. Detroit, Edgar Alpine

Larsh passed an Officer Candidate's test. During 1944 and 1945, the United States Navy sent him to college for four semesters at Villanova and Brown Universities to obtain a degree in order for him to become an officer. In June 1945, he was sent to Chapel Hill, North Carolina, for pilot training. At the conclusion of World War II in September 1945, he was discharged from the United States Navy before finishing his pilot's training or becoming an officer.

He went back home to Baltimore and later married his sweetheart, Mary Lucille Fowler, in 1946. They had five children, Karen Cecilia Larsh in 1947, Donna Ellen Larsh in 1948, Stephen Michael Larsh in 1954, Gail Ann Larsh in 1959, and William Alan Larsh in 1962. They raised their family in the suburbs of Baltimore.

Edgar Alpine Larsh became the first person in his family to obtain a college degree. He attended night school for years, finally receiving his Bachelor of Science degree from Loyola College in Baltimore, Maryland, in 1960. By 1968, he obtained a Master's degree in Liberal Arts from Johns Hopkins University. Throughout his career, he worked as a mechanical engineer at various companies in and around Baltimore, including the Glenn L. Martin Company for eighteen years, later known as Martin-

Marietta and Lockheed-Martin; the United States
Air Force as a civilian for two years;
Westinghouse Electric Corporation for four
years; and Chesapeake and Potomac Telephone
Company for eighteen years before retiring in
1988.

Edgar Alpine Larsh and Mary Lucille Larsh
had a long and happy marriage.  They were
devoted to one another, their five children and
nine grandchildren, as well as their extended
families.  Mary Lucille Larsh passed away in
1992.  Edgar Alpine Larsh died in 1998.  A year
before Edgar passed away, he gave his youngest
son, William Alan Larsh, his 1881-S United
States Liberty Head Half Eagle five-dollar gold
coin.  This coin had once belonged to Edgar's
grandfather, Leonard Ellsworth Larsh.  Leonard
reportedly carried his "lucky" five-dollar gold
piece with him his entire adult life.  The
reason this coin was so lucky for Leonard was
never revealed.  The coin was handed down
through four generations:  first by Leonard to
his son, Edgar; from Edgar to his son, Edgar
Alpine; and finally from Edgar Alpine to his
son, William.

William Alan Larsh grew up in Perry Hall,
Maryland, a suburb of Baltimore.  In 1984, he
married his high school sweetheart, Cynthia Lynn
Little.  They had two children, Ethan Edgar

Larsh in 1989 and Mary Lisabeth Larsh in 1991. William Alan Larsh worked his entire career for the Federal Bureau of Investigation (FBI) from 1984 to 2012, including almost twenty-five years as a Special Agent, transferring across the country several times during his career.

William was assigned four and a half years to the Tampa Division in Orlando, Florida; three and half years to the Washington Metropolitan Field Office in Washington, D.C.; two years to the FBI Headquarters in Washington, D.C.; a year and a half to the New Orleans Division in Shreveport, Louisiana; four and a half years to the Philadelphia Division in State College, Pennsylvania; two more years at FBI Headquarters in Washington, D.C.; and finally six and a half years to the Oklahoma City Division in Oklahoma City, Oklahoma.

William fought the battle against criminals, terrorists, and spies during his long and varied career, and was proud of his accomplishments and sacrifice. In a small way, he felt a kinship to his heroic ancestor, Paul L'Archevêque, believing that Paul's courage and perseverance combatting the perils of the early American frontier were somehow in his blood and an integral part of him too.

**Paul L'Archevêque (Larsh)**       m. Alice Dean
Born ~1734 Died 1794       Born ~1730 Died ~1787
                    Age ~60                          Age ~57


**Charles Larsh**       m. Sarah Van Swearingen
Born 1760 Died ~1815       Born 1760 Died 1849
                    Age ~55                          Age 88


**Paul Larsh**       m. Mercy Stull Minor
Born 1782 Died 1867       Born 1785 Died 1840
                    Age 84                          Age 54


**Lewis W. Larsh**       m. Mary V. Tackett
Born 1819 Died 1901       Born 1820 Died 1903
                    Age 82                          Age 83


**Leonard Ellsworth Larsh** m. Amanda C. Magneson
Born 1863 Dicd 1938       Born 1863 Died 1936
                    Age 75                          Age 72


**Edgar Larsh**       m. Elizabeth Chisholm
Born 1894 Died 1972       Born 1902 Died 1989
                    Age 77                          Age 86


**Edgar Alpine Larsh**       m. Mary Lucille Fowler
Born 1925 Died 1998       Born 1925 Died 1992
                    Age 73                          Age 66


**William Alan Larsh**       m. Cynthia Lynn Little
Born 1962       Born 1961

Larsh Family Tree

183

Paul Larsh's Last Will and Testament (P.1)
Dated November 17, 1792

Paul Larsh's Last Will and Testament (P.2)
Dated November 17, 1792

**AMANDA CHRISTINA MAGNESON LARSH**

**1863-1936**

IMMIGRATED TO THE UNITED STATES FROM SWEDEN

IN 1883

MARRIED LEONARD ELLSWORTH LARSH IN 1891

Photo taken July 1920
*LEONARD ELLSWORTH LARSH*

**1863-1938**

*AMANDA CHRISTINA MAGNESON LARSH*

*EDGAR LARSH*

1894-1972

### *THE CHISHOLM FAMILY*

ALPIN CHISHOLM (SEATED) 1858-1938; ELIZABETH
"BESSIE" CHISHOLM LARSH (STANDING) 1902-1989;
BETTY AMANDA LARSH (ON TABLE) 1921-1988; LOLITA
MARGARET LARSH (ON LAP) 1923-2000; ELIZABETH
MACDOUGALL CHISHOLM (SEATED) 1862-1929

EDGAR ALPINE LARSH

1925-1998

**MARY LUCILLE FOWLER LARSH**

**1925-1992**

*WILLIAM ALAN LARSH*

**AUTHOR**

38022970R00112

Made in the USA
Middletown, DE
11 December 2016